POINT SAL

A Story of Organized Crime, Identity Theft, Mexican Magic and Cooking

By Jonathan Schwartz

From Magic Lamp Press
Venice, California

Magic Lamp Press ™

www.legalmystery.com

This is a work of fiction. Any resemblance to actual persons, living or dead is entirely coincidental.

POINT SAL

This book, may not be reproduced in any form, stored in a retrieval system, or transmitted by any means, electronic, mechanical, by photocopying, recording, or otherwise, without written permission from the publisher, Magic Lamp Press. For permission, contact: Editor Gene Grossman at Magic Lamp Press, P.O. Box 9547, Marina del Rey, CA 90295. or gene_grossman@yahoo.com

.....

Cover photography ©MMVIII Greg Wenger
http://www.marinadelreyphotos.com/

The Tom McGuire Series
http://www.legalmystery.com

ISBN: 1-882629-83-3

1

R attlesnakes do not actually rattle; it's more of a buzz. Not a sound you'd ever forget. I woke up and realized it was my new cell phone. To stop its robotic squealing I had set it to 'vibrate,' with a fleeting lewd thought about the convergence of the telephone and the vibrator. Where's Mae West when you really need her? That night I had left the phone on the shelf by the bed, forgetting to turn it off, and when the call came in it vibrated against the varnished wood, buzzing like a rattlesnake. Four-thirty in the morning. Pulse and respiration going bananas.

"Is this Mr. McGuire?" A long-distance voice. Satellite echo, digital chop.

"Yes. It's very early here. What's up?"

"I'm calling about your new MasterCard. You've missed

the first three payments."

"I have?"

"Yes, sir." A young, somewhat educated, slightly exasperated white female with a trace of a Southern accent. Just a trace. 'Get the South out of your mouth,' that's what they say down there. If you want people to think you're smart, keep the magnolia to a minimum.

"I don't have a new MasterCard."

"Well, sir, you bought a new car on the card in Santa Barbara, California just four months ago." Smarmy and judgmental, as if she were describing a repellant sex act I had committed.

"What kind of a car?"

"A Lincoln Navigator. You should know." Now she thought I was making fun of her.

I had bought a Lincoln Navigator, that swollen pustule of a vehicle? And on a credit card? Could you even do that? The conversation had begun to assume a tone of perky irrationality I had once learned to associate with the use of expensive recreational drugs. Next she was going to tell me I had bought an elephant at the circus.

"No, ma'am, I don't own any kind of car like that." I thought she would appreciate the 'ma'am.' "Are you sure I'm the right Tom McGuire?" We ran through my mailing address, birth date, social security number.

"Is your mother's maiden name Ruth?"

"That's right. Babe Ruth."

"Well, that's what I've got here."

"The Sultan of Swat."

"Excuse me?"

It had been a family joke once, then later the image of my mother as a maiden had seemed too intimate to attach to credit applications, so I made her Ruth, first name Babe. Nobody ever said a word about it. Now someone had stolen my identity, along with my long-departed mother Babe Ruth. Not only did the joke not work any more, it made the whole thing

4

more personal.

Maria lay quietly next to me. If the call had awakened her she didn't show it. I cuddled up against her back so that we made the stacked spoons shape. Maria slept naked, and the feeling was delicious, particularly on a cold morning on a boat in C Basin. But regardless of having my arms full of sleepy naked Maria I was unable to get back to sleep. I've heard people whose homes have been robbed talk about a sense of being invaded or defiled and I realized the theft of my identity was much the same thing. Was I just a bunch of marks on a page; an array of signs and symbols, including a new SUV I didn't want? What else were they going to buy for me?

It seemed like a long time until morning. By then I had decided to be angry. At someone. I didn't know who he was just then, but I thought I could find out. He could mug at me through a thicket of internet connections, but I could sense him, smell his stinky dishonest self. He was doomed. Only Siegfried and Roy could hide a Lincoln Navigator.

This was something I could deal with. Not global warming, anthrax, school shootings, alien abductions. No, this was a particular person who had chosen me. When I found him I could hold his head down in a toilet and flush, pour seltzer up his nostrils, that kind of thing, if I had three or four really big obedient guys there to help. Not to make a joke of it. I could hurt him, take away his Lincoln Navigator. My Lincoln Navigator. Drag him behind it on a chain.

Maria awoke and I told her of my intentions.

She said "Is this a joke? Maybe someone in one of your standup workshops?"

I had been doing standup comedy workshops and showcases for years and I had learned that a lot of things civilians called jokes were really tricky ways of annoying people. But there was nobody I knew who both disliked me enough to do such a thing and had the vision to get so elaborate with it. Even Don Rickles doesn't actually smack you in the chops; it just feels like he does.

Outside the boat, sea birds were making morning noises. We were still in bed. It was Saturday morning; foggy in the Marina, warm under the covers.

I said "It's the opposite of a joke. Someone pretended to be me and bought a car. I'm upset about it."

She stretched and gave me a long look. Finally she said "Pretend it's a joke. You like jokes."

"Not when they're on me."

"Those are the best kind. If you can handle them, it shows you've got style. This hunt 'em down with a flame thrower stuff, it's not you."

I hadn't told her about the flame thrower, hadn't gotten to flame throwers yet, actually, but sometimes Maria would get ahead of me. She got up, and stood there briefly, naked in the stateroom passageway, then put on a bathrobe and went forward to the galley. Now I had to get up too. I had something to look forward to; I owned a new Lincoln. I wondered what color it was.

After a cup of coffee I got on the phone and learned that concern about my new Lincoln was not widespread. I reached a County Sheriff's Investigator whose response to my story registered somewhere between lost cat and stolen bicycle. When I told him what kind of a car it was he said "No kidding?" Identity theft was new, and a unit was being set up to deal with complaints. They'll get back to me.

2

I went to Brentwood. OJ Simpson country; San Vicente and Barrington. I knew people there who ran an olive oil store that I liked to visit. 'We're in the olive oil business,' Marlon Brando had said in *The Godfather*. In the way that life imitates art, Lou Gizzi and Victor Cannizzarro, genuine organized criminals, possibly retired, had opened an olive oil store on a good block of San Vicente Boulevard in West L.A. The neighborhood known as Brentwood.

Everyone knew they were connected. It was part of the ambiance. In case you weren't in the know, you could read it on the neon sign outside: 'La Cosa Nostra - Italian Imports.' Before they opened, when I had suggested the name was too flamboyant, Lou said "Why fart around about it? Whadda they gonna do, arrest the store?" He was right. La Cosa Nostra had flourished. Not only did it satisfy the rampant yearnings of Westside foodies, it also catered to the great American love affair with organized crime. The *Guys and Dolls* syndrome, I call it, lately reincarnated by *The Sopranos*; loveable if undereducated hoodlums, with a few bad habits. This explained their wall of celebrity head shots with inscriptions such as 'To my goombah,' from actors who felt an affinity with hoodlums because they had played them in movies. It allowed Lou Gizzi and Victor Cannizzarro to get silly prices for their exotic bottles of olive oil. Balsamic vinegar too. Hundred-year-old balsamic vinegar.

Lou smiled when I told him; he liked a good scam. "You never got bills?" he said.

"Nope."

"So they got in your mail, or they had the address changed."

"It happened three months ago. All I got was a phone call last night. This morning."

"The dealership knew what was happening."

"You think?"

He snorted. "Y'ever try and buy a new car on a credit card?"

"No. It sounds bizarre. Will they sell you a new car on a credit card?"

"Huh. Car dealers? They'll suck your dick for a quarter."

"Oh."

"A new Lincoln Navigator, that's that big humpy one, right?"

"Yeah."

"Gotta be forty, fifty grand, at least. Sure you can put it on a credit card, no problem. A new credit card, it's a little harder. But either way they're gonna read the label in your jockey shorts before you drive it away."

"You mean where it says 'fruit of the loom?'"

"Ats right." Exaggerated patience now. "And your credit report. Your bank statement, your tax return, maybe. There's a

9

lotta credit card fraud around these days."

"Tell me about it."

Gizzi was fading a little, his face was drawn, his hair more sparse than I remembered. He still wore the fat gold bracelet with 'LOU' spelled out in diamonds. Still wore the tennis-pro white cardigan and the detached dean-of-students look.

He stood behind the luxe brass and marble counter; stacks of Italian delicacies heaped up behind him. *Pannetone, amaretti, reggiano.* He seemed to be enjoying himself. It smelled cheesy in the store. The more you know about hoodlums the less romantic they seem.

We stood there dipping bread into a saucer of olive oil from a bottle you could have bought for the price of a low-end desktop computer. I asked him about his partner Victor Cannizzarro and he told me Vic took care of the cooking classes. He gestured toward the back of the store, where there was a small teaching-style kitchen.

I said "Does he still make *Conchiglie e Animelle*?

"Fuckin' A." He laughed. "He loves that shit."

"Scallops and sweetbreads, right?"

Lou looked at me intently. How did I know this about his partner? In fact, they had kidnapped me once, on the 405 Freeway, and talked with me about scallops and sweetbreads, among other subjects. Now Lou didn't remember. I damn well remembered.

I said "I noticed you got an A.'"

"What?"

"The restaurant Nazis gave you an 'A.'"

"Oh, in the front window. The health people. Yeah. They asked me do I have rats. Y'imagine? I'm gonna tell them I got rats so they can stick 'em up my ass?"

"You've got rats?"

"Hey, the world's fulla rats. You want a favor or what?" He corked the bottle of Panne Olio we had been sampling. "Talk about rats, after we opened one time we found a bug in here. A

10

real one. Those jerks downtown think somebody's gonna talk business in an olive oil store called Cosa Nostra?" He snorted. "We put it over by the cappuccino machine. Anybody wanted to say anything we turned on the steam. All they were gonna hear was 'whoosh, whoosh'."

He motioned me toward the back of the store, where twenty or so folding chairs were arranged in front of a stainless steel stovetop and kitchen counter. Copper cookware hung from a rack. Where Brentwood ladies learned to cook, doo-dah, doo-dah.

Tonight, according to the chalkboard on the back wall, the celebrated Italian Chef Victor Cannizzarro would do *Spigola Alla Procidana*, striped bass with red wine vinegar and mint. There was a professional head shot of Vic smiling in his chef's toque. The last time I had seen a photograph of Victor Cannizzarro I was employed at the US Attorney's Office. He was scowling in that picture and there had been booking numbers on a little sign around his neck. Then he wasn't a chef, he was a crook, but I remember later he told me he was taking cooking lessons. So now he's a chef. I pictured him pounding veal with a serious look and a cigar in his mouth.

Lou said "So waddiya want, the car? The guys?"

"Right now all I want is the location."

"You're gonna go there?"

"Maybe. Depends on where it is."

Lou smiled. "You're gonna play with them? You might ought to be a little careful, you being a lawyer and all." He looked at me thoughtfully. "I didn't know you better I'd say you were pissed off."

I thought about flame-throwers. "Better to be pissed off than pissed on."

3

"**Y**ou paid fifty-five dollars for this?" Maria held up a cunningly wrought long-necked bottle of Balsamic de Montefiori.

"There's a seventy-five dollar bottle of olive oil in there too."

We sat in the salon of my forty-eight-foot Chris-Craft liveaboard home, *Den Mother*. Outside was blue water, weak winter sunshine and boats. Inside, Maria scowled at my assortment of Italian delicacies. She had been the eldest of six children. All of them had worked part time in the family grocery store in the San Gabriel Valley. Her parents' store was in a working-class neighborhood and had not carried the kinds of products Lou Gizzi and Victor Cannizzarro sold to the Brentwood ladies. She made a sour face as each item emerged from the bag.

"White anchovies? What are they for?"

I didn't exactly know. Sometimes when I get into one of those little specialty stores I go into a trance. She held up a package of imported nougat with hazelnuts, each piece wrapped with a different brightly lithographed picture of a saint. Italian baseball cards.

"For me?"

I nodded. She hadn't asked what it cost. I said "You collect a complete set of saints they give you free liposuction."

She looked annoyed and stood up. She was wearing a yellow cashmere turtleneck sweater and low-rider denims. Which went well with her jet-black hair and toasty skin. Over the years I had come to understand that Maria was a lot smarter than I was, but a whole lot more forgiving. She was also the most intensely female person I had ever met. There were no women like that when I was growing up; none that I knew about. If my mother had ever met Maria she would have died on the spot, or threatened to. She looked at me with mock-innocent confusion and said "Liposuction?

"Nothing personal. It was an Italian joke. Forget it."

From her expression I could tell she didn't so much forget it as file it away for possible use later. The people you've got watch out for are the ones who never throw anything away.

She said "What were you asking them?"

"Huh?"

"It's the Lincoln, isn't it?"

"Can't I just buy olive oil sometimes?"

She opened one of the little blocks of nougat. "Buy all the olive oil you want. Rub it on the soles of your feet if you want to. But don't lie to me."

"I just asked him if they could locate the car, that's all."

"Which one did you ask, the short fat smelly one with the cigar or the freeze-dried Tony Bennett type with the dime-store diamond bracelet?"

"You know their names."

"Their names are shit, Tom."

13

We had had this discussion before. When I was a kid, busily running on the educational treadmill middle-class parents force on their kids, maybe somebody should have been teaching me how to steal cars. I had a Jewish mother, who took religious observance and instruction seriously, and an Irish Catholic father who practiced labor law, kept out of the way and stayed out late a lot. I grew up with prescription glasses that would get lost, a never-ending schedule of obligations; regular school, religious school (Jewish and Catholic, at different stages; a story in itself), clarinet, homework, pimples, masturbation. I had wanted karate, which was available after school in the gym, but clarinet won. My mother said karate was for hoodlums. So that was it for me, except for a season of shoplifting until the store detectives got me. The clarinet got lost on the subway.

Maria's experience had been different. Her father had kept a loaded revolver under the counter in the bodega. It was what shopkeepers did in a working-class neighborhood in the San Gabriel Valley. Her brothers would sneak in and borrow the gun after hours and, when they had the time, teach their big sister how to shoot. The eldest boy was shot dead in a street confrontation between rival gangs. Maria had no romantic illusions about violence. She did have a collection of six or eight handguns. She took them to pistol ranges and shot them regularly. She said it calmed her down.

Maria gathered up the Italian delicacies and took them down to the galley to put away. My little jars and bottles.

"Actually," I said, "I was thinking of taking one of their cooking classes."

She looked up at me from the galley; rolled her eyes. "*No te va a servir para nada.*"

Except for 'nada,' the words were not familiar, but I didn't need to know Spanish to understand her. It sounded the same when my mother used to say it in Yiddish: '*De darfts dus vie a loch in kopf.*' You need it like a hole in the head.

14

*   *   *

It had been quite some time after I met Maria that I realized she had two degrees from UCLA. In the beginning she had played it straight San Gabriel Valley local girl. She had been wary of me, an Irish-Jewish older guy from New York, probably more exotic to her than she appeared to me, and from a place she had never been. Did I think of her then as Carmen Miranda, dancing the conga with a flowing skirt and fruit on her hat? You know, 'ay-yi-yi-yi-yi I like you varrrr-y much.' Yeah, of course I had thought that. Just a little. But what might have been a culture clash resolved into a game. Part of my respect for her came from a feeling I had that on some level she might be a bigger smartass than I was.

4

Each day when I drove to work I would notice a Lincoln Navigator on almost every block. At one point I thought I saw three in a row, waiting for a light. It was like a Hitchcock movie where the main character is frantically looking for someone in a grey fedora and suddenly realizes every man on the street is wearing one. You can't count on reality to be neutral; sometimes it'll wake up, get interested, and start playing with you. When I saw the familiar outline in traffic I would try to pull alongside, see who was driving. The drivers were all harmless-looking, except for one dead-on sleazy mutt; just the type. He noticed me staring at him and looked worried; turned at the next corner. No pursuit.

In the office I had a long marginally polite telephone conversation with a fraud investigator from MasterCard. Mr.

Mahmoud. He kept asking me if I was sure that I had not charged the Lincoln on the card, or had something to do with it. He pointed out that a car dealership would ask for supporting identification in such a transaction, which I said sounded reasonable. After a good deal of this I said I didn't appreciate his insinuations and he said he wasn't insinuating, drawing the five syllables out slowly, as if some greater threat had been intended.

Lou Gizzi called after lunch. "You want the car, it's in San Diego."

"That was fast."

"Yeah, well, when this kind of stuff happens the cars usually go south, so that's where I asked about it."

"Usually?"

A pause. "Look, Tommy, you asked me a question, so I'm telling you." He gave me a San Diego street address and a vehicle license, which I wrote down. "The people involved, they're like amateurs, except they don't think so. They won't appreciate you coming around. Best thing for you is, give this stuff to your credit card people, let them carry the ball."

"Right. And where do I tell them I got the information?"

He snorted. "Fuck do I know? Tell 'em you've got a connection with the Mob."

There was no way I could explain it; I didn't buy the car but I knew where it was. What was my next move? I bounced it off a couple of friends of mine in phone calls that afternoon, and the best anyone could come up with was that if I really knew where the car was I could call it in stolen, except it was never actually stolen, or at least not stolen from me. Except kind of. They all told me not to get involved.

*   *   *

At dinner Maria said "Don't go there."

"Where?"

"San Diego."

17

"Did I say I wanted to go there?"

"No, but you do. It's obvious."

We were back on Standard Time and it was full dark out in the channel. Energetic drunks were making festive noises on a large yacht just across the channel from us.

I knew Maria was just trying to protect me, but I kept coming back to the Babe Ruth stuff, my mother's made-up maiden name on some asshole's credit application. My mother could deal out swift punishment when it was deserved. She wasn't called the Sultan of Swat for nothing.

Maria said "Cars are middle-class bullshit, Tom. They're what Americans are supposed to have instead of lives."

She was right. I remembered something I had heard in a TV commercial: 'Here it is, the car you've been dreaming of.' What kind of dipshit dreams about a car? When I dream, I can fly or I'm having intimate encounters with strange women. Things like that. Never cars.

I said "So I ignore the whole thing? Just sit here and let them stick it to me like a big lump of play-doh?"

"Play-doh?"

"It's like clay. You didn't play with it when you were a kid?"

She squinted at me, ate a little more dinner, took a sip of wine. I had bought an Australian lobster tail and she had cut it up and stir-fried it with chopped ginger, fresh water chestnuts, sherry, served it over basmati.

"No, *Señor*," she said, in a stage-Mexican accent I have traced to the character Poncho in the Cisco Kid TV series. "We do not play with the clay, we need it for to make the pots."

"Two degrees from UCLA and listen to you."

She lowered her eyes. "Jess, I know," then dropped the act. "OK, if you want we can go down there together."

"On the bike? You know what that does to me."

Maria rode a Harley. I have explained to her she is overcompensating for the role she had to play growing up, *mamacita* to a large working family, but there you are. People

18

insist on doing what they want. Same as with the handguns. I had pointed out to her that it was a serious crime to carry a loaded gun around on your motorcycle. She had sniffed at me. Disdainfully. And this is someone with a responsible job with the County Department of Adult Protective Services. Maria has told me I'm too conservative. Chickenshit, actually, was what she said, but I don't think she meant it harshly.

It's just that I practice law, and people pay me for my advice. I suppose it's hard for me to understand why another person wouldn't want me to run their life for them.

When I go somewhere with her on the Harley, I'm the one who rides in back. 'Riding bitch' the bikers call it. Soon after we first met we spent a day together on the bike, going up Pacific Coast Highway and then Topanga Canyon, stopping here and there. I had never been on a motorcycle before. I'm not sure Maria was trying to scare me but there were moments of sheer terror.

The problem turned out to concern my testicles. Not metaphorically, as in was I macho enough, but anatomically. When I took a shower late that afternoon, I was shocked to find that a familiar part of my body had moved without leaving a forwarding address. My testicles had disappeared. After some investigation I figured out where the little critters had gone, and encouraged them to return. I've had it explained to me by a doctor. A fairly common response to danger or extreme cold, he said. The testicles migrate back up the inguinal canal, which is how they got where they belong in the first place. It has never happened to me again, but it's not the kind of thing you look forward to. Long after the event, I made the mistake of telling Maria about it. *La migracion de los huevos*, she called it.

5

The address Lou had given me turned out to be east of downtown San Diego in a hilly residential neighborhood dating from the early 1900's. Bungalow-style cottages and larger two or three story Carpenter Gothic homes that must have been gorgeous when new. Hispanic working class giving way to younger more monied downtown types. Or so it seemed. People stared at us as we went by, but then people stare at anyone on a Harley because the machine is intentionally designed to make an unbelievably loud, obnoxious noise.

There was no Lincoln Navigator at the address Lou had given me. It was a well-kept old white stucco house on a corner. There was a garage on the property, the door pulled shut, but it was 1920's era construction; far too small to hold the Lincoln. In the front yard an old man in coveralls and a straw hat was

21

poking at sparse hedges with a gardener's shears. Maria dismounted, spoke to him briefly, then returned. The Lincoln and its owner, she said, were in Tijuana. He went there often, on business.

It pissed me off. "Sure," I said, "He's down at *Cien Años* eating a big meal he's going to charge to me, then he'll drive home in my Lincoln."

Maria had agreed to ride down with me subject to a number of concessions, among them that I would not attempt any direct engagement of the foe; reconnaissance only. In this way were my grim fantasies of revenge treated as an excuse for a weekend frolic, an excursion on the Harley.

*   *   *

It turned out to be a piece of cake. The SUV was parked on *Calle Segunda* not far off *Avenida Benito Juarez*, where it loomed in the busy late afternoon of Tijuana's louche urban scene, looking as if it had fallen there from the sky. Black. Tan leather. Dealer's paper plate. Doors unlocked, key in the ignition. I took a quick look over my shoulder at Maria straddling the bike, and got in the driver's seat. Piece of cake.

I started it up and pulled away from the curb. I'm sure Maria was furious with me but I couldn't see her expression under the motorcycle helmet faceplate. Probably a good thing. I waited in line at the border, Maria behind me on the Harley. At last, I was having fun. I tuned in a jazz station on the FM. Better sounds than I had at home. Intense new car smell; the smell of money. I waved at the border guards as I drove through the checkpoint and across the border. They waved back. I have that kind of face.

The fun wore off as we convoyed through downtown San Diego in the slow lane; me riding point, Maria behind, heading north on the San Diego Freeway. I started thinking about the checkpoint ahead at San Clemente and wondering who would leave his shiny new Lincoln Navigator unlocked with the keys in

22

the ignition on the street in downtown TJ unless he wanted to get it stolen. I signaled and took the next offramp, pulling in to a fast-food establishment and parking in a far corner of the lot. Maria pulled in next to me. Once out of her helmet she gave me her best death-ray look. Stealing the Lincoln had not been in the script, but all she said was "You want one of these burgers?"

"No. You got a screwdriver?"

Of course she had a screwdriver. Hell, she had a .357 Magnum, didn't she? Her puzzlement lasted until I removed a large piece of interior trim from the right front door, exposing a neat stack of fat plastic bags. One could assume the whole goddamn thing was stuffed to the gills with dope. My lovely SUV.

Maria said "Cover that up," which I immediately did. There was an impulse to run like hell, and we both looked at the Harley.

"No," I said. "The thing's in my name. We can't just leave it here."

She did a slow pan around the parking lot. Nothing out of the ordinary seemed to be going on.

She said "Let's go in and get a cup of coffee."

"I don't want a cup of coffee."

"Maybe you'll change your mind."

She grabbed my arm firmly and walked me in. We got coffees at the counter and sat where we could see our vehicles in the gathering darkness.

I said "I was set up. We're fucked."

Maria said "Drink your coffee."

As we sat, two young men in leather jackets walked past the window, each putting on what looked like a pair of red rubber dishwashing gloves. Kitchen staff, I would have thought, except that they walked straight to the Lincoln and entered it. Then its lights came on, and it started moving down the parking lane in front of the window where we sat. As it passed in front of us a hand emerged from the passenger side window and waved us a red rubber goodbye.

I lurched in my seat and had a brief insane impulse to jump up and yell something like 'Hey, that's my car. They're stealing my car,' or some such, then I regained a little clarity and looked across the table at Maria, who was wearing an I-told-you-so smirk.

"There's no pleasing some people," she said. "You wanted to find it so badly, an hour later you want to get rid of it. Now someone takes it off your hands and you don't like that either."

"They were watching us the whole time."

"*Si. Claro.*"

"They knew we were coming?"

She drew a long breath, and I realized the day had not been a picnic for her either. "Who told you to come down here, Tom?"

Lou Gizzi, of course, that was who.

6

If you want to know how it feels to have an extremely large sports utility vehicle full of cocaine, or maybe heroin, out there somewhere registered in your name, with your fingerprints on it, a vehicle that you yourself drove into the United States across an international border, think of the newspaper stories you have read about giant asteroids predicted to be on a collision course with Earth. Federal minimum sentencing guidelines would finish me off as efficiently as any giant asteroid, and I had the same amount of control over the process.

There was nothing to do but return to the Marina. The optimistic spirit of adventure with which we had begun the journey was now absent, replaced with world-class dread. Would they be waiting for us? And which 'they?' What if the

Lincoln was there, parked in the lot by our dock? Wouldn't that be cute? These were the people I was going to drag behind the car on a chain.

Clever little radio intercoms in our helmets made conversation possible on the bike. Somewhere around San Onofre I said "Why would the Z's do this to me?" The reference was to Gizzi and Cannizzarro, names with so many z's in them that, taken together, they had always reminded me of the sound of a dentist's drill.

Maria said "Maybe this will cure you of your Jesse James syndrome."

"It's the *Guys and Dolls* syndrome."

"Whatever. It's what I've been afraid of for years; one day your exotic friends are going to cut you up and feed you to the birds."

"No. We go back. They wouldn't use me for a mule. If they ever wanted to put the squeeze on me it would be something much more artistic than driving drugs across the border. There must be plenty of schmucks they can get to do that."

It didn't occur to me at the time, but that thought is probably what the schmuck thinks as he's driving the drugs across the border. I had bought my own bullshit.

Maria said "Have you figured out the rubber gloves?"

"You mean the guys that took the Lincoln? I guess they didn't want to leave fingerprints."

"Good. What else?"

"What?"

"Well, if they were being so careful then, what do you think the chances are the car was wiped clean when they left it in TJ?"

"Oh....shit."

"See what I mean?"

"The only fingerprints in there are mine."

Radio silence. We passed the huge twin concrete breasts of the San Onofre nuclear electric generating plant. Every time I drive by I wait for them to explode.

Maria said "So, in your opinion your friends have too much respect for you to screw you in a common drug deal; they would give you a more upscale screwing." She may have shook her head; it's hard to tell with the motorcycle helmet. "Anyway, you can ask them about it tomorrow night."

"Tomorrow night?"

"It's your first cooking class."

*   *   *

Victor Cannizzarro was explaining antipasto. He was wearing a complete set of chef's whites, with toque. On the left-hand side of his chest was embroidered the phrase 'La Cosa Nostra,' and in smaller letters 'Brentwood, California.' He was clean shaven for so late in the day, and without a cigar for the first time since I remembered interviewing him in a holding cell at the Metropolitan Detention Center, downtown. Cigars are not allowed in jail. He stood behind a broad table that included a stove, sink and work surface; a short, intense man in his sixties, considerably overweight. But without the cigar, in chef's whites with a fresh shave, not bad at all. Anthony Bourdain kinda opened the door to weirdos in the kitchen. Nobody was complaining.

Above, a large mirror hung from the ceiling at an angle, so spectators could look down at the work in progress.

"With your antipasto," Vic was saying to a respectful group of about twenty-five, seated on folding chairs in front of him, "you don't get to do much to it. So you're gonna start with the best. You're gonna put a little of everything, so everybody gets something they like. You make a nice antipasto and somebody says he don't like it, throw him outta the house. He's not serious."

Nervous laughter. He was doing ok, considering his background, but he was no Julia Child.

"Get good Genoa salami," Vic said, holding up a salami.

27

"Buy from Italians. Same with cheese. Buy it here. Whatever it is, if you get it in an Italian deli you're gonna be ok. And forget about putting fresh vegetables. Some people put carrot sticks." He winced. "Carrot sticks, like you're gonna feed to a horse. You're gonna put vegetables in your antipasto you make *Giardinera*, means you cut them small and blanche them, then marinate them overnight in vinegar, serve them with oil. I gotta sheet here for *Giardinera*. Get one before you leave. You wanna add anchovies to your antipasto, maybe olives? Buy 'em right here. Best you gonna get outside a New York."

He went on, talking about *Frittata, Suppli, Aringa Marinata*. He seemed to know his stuff. As he spoke I surveyed the group. I had been to a few cooking demonstration classes with Maria. You get young women who want to learn, older married women with money and time on their hands, once in a while a bachelor or divorced dad who would like to be able to show off for a girlfriend or child on Court-ordered visitation, and foodies like me and Maria, for whom hunting, gathering and cooking had become a serious avocation. About half the people in attendance fit the pattern. The rest of them most definitely did not. What we had was a group of young men in their twenties or thirties who seemed to know each other. Not a bowling league, not a Bible study group or soccer team. No. Wiseguys, definitely. A little too much jewelry, shoes nobody could afford, uncomfortably earnest expressions. Good suits or expensive leather jackets. Too dressy for a cooking class, even in Brentwood.

They sat respectfully, listening to Cannizzarro talk about antipasto, then segue into *Spaghetti con Fegatini de Pollo,* which he cooked from start to finish before our admiring eyes. The idea of chicken livers in spaghetti had never appealed to me before. Now, I figured maybe I would give it a chance.

When he got to *Aragosta Piccante* things got seriously weird. From under the counter Cannizzarro produced what looked like a five-pound live Maine lobster. Oohs and Aahs from the gallery. It was the liveliest lobster I had ever seen, and seemed intent on returning to its native waters as soon as possible. To restrain it, Cannizzarro placed it under an inverted wire dish drainer, where it rattled around ineffectually. Its claws were not bound by the rubber bands you usually see, and it snapped at the wires of the dish drainer. As interesting as this was to the group, it galvanized the wiseguy contingent. There was a drawing together and general focusing of attention. They stared at the lobster as if Cannizzarro had pulled it out of his hat. They slid glances at each other. This, whatever it was, was what they had come tonight to witness.

Cannizzarro reached under the wire dish drainer and picked up the lobster, holding it by its back. It waved its legs and snapped its claws. He stared at the group, a serious expression on his face, saying nothing for a beat, two beats, three beats. The lobster squirmed, its image reflected in the mirror overhead. Nobody moved.

"This guy," Cannizzarro said, gesturing toward his captive, "he's an old man. He's been around a long time, right?"

Now, surprisingly, there were murmurs of assent from the young wiseguys. Nods of the head, which Cannizzarro acknowledged.

"Now," he continued, "how does an old guy like this live? Where does he dip his beak?" He paused a moment. "In the sea around him, that's where." More murmurs of agreement. "And what does he give back for what he gets? He works the bottom a the sea; he helps keep things clean. Capische?"

I had the sense that the regular West Side attendees, the foodies, bored housewives and the rest, were not tracking this. But the wiseguy contingent was eating it up. Grinning, giving each other the high sign.

Cannizzarro held the lobster higher. His voice rose. "What happens when this guy forgets to give in exchange for what he gets? Anybody want to say forget it? Anyone want to say save this lobster, put him back inna water, let him go back to doin' what he's been doin'?"

Silence. Head shaking from the young wiseguys, glazed

29

nervous looks from the rest of us.

"Ok then," said Cannizzarro. His eyes gleamed. He reached under the counter, produced a cleaver, and pierced the lobster through the head, killing it instantly. Two women got up and left. Wiseguys applauded. The rest of us looked at each other. I didn't think any of the civilians there wanted to make *Aragosta Piccante* that badly. Cannizzarro cracked the lobster in various places, and went on to cook it, reassemble it on a plate, then dress it with a sauce he had just made and garnish it with parsley. Several more Brentwood ladies bailed out during this process.

By the time the class was over, only about half of us were left; a few of the women, me and all the young wiseguys, who were now helping Cannizzarro fold up the chairs and clean and put away the cooking utensils. Looking at him I realized he had developed a chef's persona to go with the costume. You would never guess that he had once chained some miserable soul to a water pipe and tortured him with lit cigarettes. At the US Attorney's office we thought it was funny, since his victim was another hoodlum. Let them all kill each other was our motto, though not for publication. We were a cynical lot.

Watching Lou wield his cleaver I recalled an unattributed murder of one of our most useful informants, a messy business involving decapitation followed by defenestration. No proof, but at the time it had sounded to us like Cannizzarro's work.

I thought that the seeds of the trouble Maria and I had experienced in Mexico and San Diego must have come from Cannizzarro or his partner, at least the Tijuana part. It had all been too neat. But looking at Cannizzarro stacking folding chairs with a crowd of his admiring young street captains I realized I couldn't bring it up. In the past, I had been the law enforcement guy; Mr. kick-ass. I had tried to be as nice as possible in the role, but there are certain limitations. My office had indicted and convicted Cannizzarro and sent him to prison for five years. True I had not been lead counsel but I had worked on the case. That had been his second fall. The first time he went up it was out of Denver and I had nothing to do with it; wasn't even in the Government at the time, but it seemed unlikely that Cannizzarro would appreciate these subtle distinctions, and he had had at least five years to think about it. He was aware I was in the class tonight, but, clearly, he had not been thrilled to see me. I had a sense that this was not the time to give Cannizzarro the advantage by asking him for something. It must be like lion taming; it only gets dangerous when they forget who's got the whip. Or if you left the whip at home.

I realized as I got in my car that I had forgotten to take a copy of the recipe for *Giardiniera.*

7

As I entered the parking lot at the Marina I checked the area for Lincoln Navigators; thought I saw one but it turned out to be a Dodge. The whole thing was getting ridiculous. As Maria had said, first I wanted to find the Lincoln, now I was afraid of it; was afraid of all of them; any of them, actually. I passed my dock and went on to the next one. There, on the end tie, was *More Gefilte Fish*, Murray Markoff's beautiful fifty-two foot twin-diesel Elliott.

Murray was retired, a former bookmaker. A kindly little old grandfather by appearance, a depths-of-Brooklyn street guy when he opened his mouth. Murray spoke the kind of regional speech we're going to miss in a couple of generations when everyone speaks the language like a network news anchor. One day, the Library of Congress will send Murray some earnest graduate student with a tape recorder to preserve the sound of Brooklyn English; the sound of places like Greenpoint, Red Hook, Sheepshead Bay. 'Dere wus thoity doity poiple boids...' Close enough to home to remind me of a childhood in the Bronx.

Murray was short and bald, except for a fringe of white hair, and, like everybody else around here, deeply tanned. In retirement in Southern California he had adopted the customs of the country, and dressed in faded jeans and one or another of a large collection of Aloha shirts. Murray was a liveaboard, like me. His first boat, the original *Gefilte Fish*, sank in spectacular circumstances during the previous annual Marina del Rey Christmas Boat Parade. This may not have been an accident, although the actual cause of the sinking was disputed. Murray had been pulled from the water by the Harbor Patrol. *Gefilte Fish* was lost, but Murray had dined out on the story ever since. Over the years he had been able to put aside a lot of money, due in part to the tech bubble and some strange things that had happened to me in which Murray had been involved. So, the fifty-two foot twin diesel Elliott, a vessel so fine you'll hardly ever see one amidst the clutter of Tupperware that fills most marinas in Southern California.

Murray was aboard, and we sat out on deck and talked for awhile. I described the adventures we had with the Lincoln Navigator.

He said "It was anybody but you, Tom, I'd say it didn't happen."

"I wish."

He puffed on his cigar and looked speculatively at the night sky over C Basin. "Yeah. Well, y'know, wish in one hand, shit in the other..."

"I know. See which one fills up faster."

"Those Italians," he said, "they're not going to do anything for you. I dunno why you even go down there."

"I buy things for the kitchen. You like what I cook."

He snorted. "What's wrong with the grocery store? No,

33

not Tommy. He's gotta go to a special place, spend a fortune on stuff no one ever heard of." A pause. "Those high-class crooks of yours..." He flipped the remains of his cigar into the water. "You wanna shoot some pool?"

Ownership of a first-class powerboat did not mean that Murray went to sea very often. When the salesman had first shown him the boat he had emphasized its size by remarking, merely as a figure of speech, that the salon was roomy enough to accommodate a pool table. Murray had been taken by the idea, and had installed a regulation Brunswick pool table in the salon, as well as a small bar at the forward end, where the dining area had been. Six barstools. This against the advice of everyone he knew, (as to the pool table; everyone had been in favor of the bar), all of whom had pointed out that, ideally, a pool table should not be capable of tilting, which his would be apt to do in any kind of weather. To these people Murray pointed out that he didn't plan to take the boat to sea very often, that the possible pitching or rolling of the table would only be an issue while a game was in progress, and that the small amount of motion likely while the boat was at the end-tie would make things more interesting. The pool table could not have fit through any hatch, and had to be assembled in the salon. It was through-bolted to the cabin sole, which had required reinforcement. Due to its extreme weight if it ever got loose in heavy weather it would probably destroy the boat. As it was, every time Murray took *More Gefilte Fish* out in the Bay all the barstools always fell over.

Murray racked the balls and selected a cue.

"People complain about this table," he said. "But usually people who play here are half in the bag anyway. You're gonna drink and shoot pool, why should you complain if the table tilts a little? I mean, be realistic; you drink enough, everything starts to tilt, right?" I agreed that this was so. "Anyway, if your shot goes toward the front of the boat or the back of the boat, it's not so bad. Maybe it'll veer off a little. You shoot from side to side, sometimes the cue ball will stop, then roll back to you.

That's a problem."

We played Eight-Ball for a while.

Murray said "You think you wanna be a crook?"

"What?"

"The excitement. Look, when I was workin', everything we did was against the law. If it was numbers or booking bets, you could get arrested any time. You had to collect from somebody who lost a lotta dough, it could be dangerous. Even when we had the cops workin' for us, you still couldn't trust them. It kept you on your toes. Now please don't be offended I'm saying this, but in my opinion you're not cut out for it."

"You're telling me I'd make a lousy crook?"

He shrugged. "You wanna put it that way. I mean, look at your track record."

The wind had come up a little. and we stood and watched my last shot make a slow semicircle across the green felt.

Murray said "Tom, you're a lawyer. You know better. This cockamamie car, it's not yours. Never was. A bunch of bunco guys get together with a bent car dealer to rip off a bank, what's it to you?

"They stole my identity, Murray. They knew my mother's maiden name."

This stopped him. "Your mother? What was her maiden name?"

"Babe Ruth."

"I didn't know you had baseball players in your family." He smiled. "My aunt was Phil Rizzuto."

"Ok, so it wasn't her real name. We called her the Sultan of Swat because if she didn't like what you were doing she'd bop you one."

"So you were an abused child?"

"Don't be silly. It just made me mad that they knew the name."

"And this is why you steal cars and drive drugs across the border and nobody's even paying you to do it?" He turned to look out at the channel, addressing his remarks to someone out there. "This is not a crook. A schmuck, maybe."

"That's harsh.

"Harsh? I dunno from harsh, but I can recognize a good old-fashioned cluster-fuck when I see one. Lookit you," pointing at me with his pool cue, "can't go back to the Italians because you can't trust them, don't wanna give them the satisfaction and 'cause you figure they're just gonna play with you some more. Can't go to the cops 'cause first thing you tell them you drove in a load of drugs they're gonna arrest you."

He called the four-ball, shot and missed. "You're not a player, Tom."

"Till now, I never thought it was going to be much of an issue."

"Yeah, but you dance around it; I've seen you."

"I'd like to sit this one out."

"You wish." He chuckled. "If that Lincoln turns up fulla drugs with your prints on it you'll be doin' the Navigator Fandango."

36

8

The next morning Larry Hayden called me at the office. Larry and I had been prosecutors together in the Los Angeles office of the United States Attorney, a long time ago. I spent a couple of years finding out I wasn't comfortable there, but it had suited Larry just fine. He had risen in the ranks, had a fancy title, and now regarded me with the holier-than-thou resentment that such people reserve for former civil service lawyers who have managed to escape the sticky clutches of Government. If you asked him, we were friends, although he had once had me arrested.

"I didn't know you liked to cook," he said.

"What?"

"You like to cook."

"It's against the law?"

"We saw you at the cooking class last night."

Silence. I was glad he was on the phone and not sitting in my office where he could have seen my face.

I said "Wait a minute, Larry, could we start this conversation over?" There's nothing like a guilty mind to put you on the defensive. "I'm under surveillance?"

"If you were, you think I'd call and tell you about it?"

"Please, get to the point. I've got stuff to do here."

"It's not you, it's the store."

"La Cosa Nostra?"

"Right."

"Things must be slow at your shop."

"Never been busier."

"Well, Maria is always telling me it's a crime what they charge."

"Heh, heh, heh." His laugh was a soft bleating sound, like a polite little billy goat. Humor did not take up much space in Larry's world. "We're not actually watching the store, except once in a while. And by the way, it's not a secret. They came out and gave our guys cannolli once. No, last night we had three different O.C. guys under surveillance and they all turned up at La Cosa Nostra."

"And went to cooking class?"

"Who knows? We couldn't follow them into the store. You were there. What did they do?"

"Cooking class."

"You learn anything?"

"Yeah. I learned that no matter where you go Uncle fucking Sam is watching you."

"Aah, you already knew that, Tom. Price you pay to live in a free society. Look, here's why I called. We're wondering if you could keep an eye on Cannizzarro, tell us what he does in class."

"Why don't you get a Judge to let you put a bug in there?"

"We tried. He didn't like our affidavit. He said it's not a

crime to make Italian food."

"The man has a point. Was it Judge Carlucci?"

"How'd you know?"

"I'm psychic. But you really are wasting your time." I drew a deep breath; the conversation wasn't turning out as badly as I had feared. "Ok, in the first place I'm not going to do it, but there's nothing there. He made antipasto; he made spaghetti with chicken livers."

"Gross."

"Suit yourself. He made spicy lobster. We watched. We got a little taste of everything.

"You've been to these things before?"

"A few."

"And you didn't notice anything out of the ordinary last night?

I thought of Victor Cannizzarro, two-time convicted felon, all in white, holding the huge struggling lobster in one hand, the cleaver in the other.

"No."

*   *   *

They say whenever you need a cop there's never one around. Unfortunately, this also works in reverse. Shortly after I hung up on Larry Hayden I had a visit from Investigator Sheldon Morse of the LA County Sheriff's Department. Investigator Morse said he was with the identity theft unit. In fact, he said that he was the identity theft unit, which was new and having difficulty getting staffed amid County-wide budget cutting.

He sat across from me in one of my client chairs, looking out the window at the docks of Marina del Rey with obvious appreciation.

"Got a hell of a view." he said. I agreed.

"Not much we're gonna be able to do for you."

"No?"

"The vehicle was purchased in Santa Barbara. It's the only lead we have. You live here. I'm not going to go up there to investigate, even if we had the personnel. Best we can do is send it up to the Santa Barbara DA's investigators. Maybe we can put out an APB for the car, put it on the hot sheet."

This was not what I wanted to hear. "Well, it's not my car, so I can't report it stolen."

He squinted at me. "Technically it's not stolen, right."

"So let the bank report it."

"What's it to you, Mr... uh..." He looked down at his notebook for my name; didn't find it. This was the guy who was going to help me find my stolen identity.

I said "McGuire."

"Thank you. McGuire."

"I don't care about the car," I heard myself say, "it's the people who did it. Find them."

"You don't care about the car?" I had said the wrong thing, but Investigator Morse seemed to be running on autopilot. He shrugged, made a couple of entries in his notebook, folded up his papers and departed. He'd get back to me.

*　　*　　*

It was impossible to get anything done. Running a solo law practice is a little like playing a violin solo; if you're not in the mood, better keep the whole thing to yourself because you don't have a symphony orchestra behind you to play loud and cover up your mistakes. Worse, somebody had parked a black Lincoln Navigator across the street from my office, where I could see it from my window. Pulling the shades made no difference to the stomach-shriveling effect it had on me. After the third time I peeked through the shades at this icon of my own personal doom I gave up and went back to the boat, where I busied myself on the foredeck, sorting out fouled ground tackle in the chain locker. I was standing up there when I heard the sound of Maria's Harley in the parking lot. When the end of the world comes, it will sound like a Harley-Davidson.

Maria did not consider Investigator Morse to be much of an issue.

"I work for the County, Tom. I hear things. There are years of identity theft complaints. Nobody's ever done anything."

She was wearing her go-to-the-office getup; little blue suit over a serious-minded brassiere, black pumps, French braid. She had boots she wore on the bike. The pumps rode in a leather satchel over the rear wheel, nestled in together with the .357 Magnum. I stood in the stateroom and watched her change clothes, enjoying the transformation as her middle-management garb was replaced by little shaggy cutoff jeans and a tee-shirt on which the Eiffel Tower was depicted in sequins. No bra. We had bought the shirt on the Rue de Rivoli the year before. I couldn't imagine being without her.

"When you take off that bra," I said, "they come bounding out like a couple of puppies that have been shut up in the house all day."

"You're weird."

"Who says?"

"My mother, for one."

"What else does she say?"

"She wants to know why we don't get married."

"What do you tell her?"

She thought for a moment. "I tell her that she's got eleven grandchildren from my brothers' families and the boat's too small for raising kids. And that you're weird."

I stood behind her, hugging her puppies. "What's the real reason?

"Things happen when they're supposed to happen."

"That's ancient Hispanic wisdom?"

"UCLA. Undergraduate course in Eastern religions. You're Carmen Mirandizing me again."

It was true. There were Puerto Ricans in New York when

41

I was growing up, plenty of them in the public schools I attended, but the only person in my life I was sure was Mexican was Carmen Miranda, who could be heard singing about bananas on records my mother would play. Nobody told me Carmen Miranda was Brazilian. After I first encountered Maria, in a shocking instant-attraction moment, I came to realize I had a lifetime collection of stereotypes on the subject of Mexicans and Mexico. Reality tended to wear away this material, as I got to know Maria and her family, but we had too much fun with it to give up entirely on Ignorant-Gringo-meets-Chiquita-Banana.

She held out a letter. "I stopped for the mail on the way down. Here's something for you from Santa Barbara Lincoln Mercury."

"Who?"

"You want some ancient Hispanic advice?"

"Sure."

"Don't open it."

9

"What's a remote keyless entry with panic button?"
"I told you not to open it."

I handed her the letter. I had opened it against her advice. I would compromise by not reading it "I think it's a recall notice. What are they talking about?"

She studied it for a moment. "Well, remote keyless entry, that sounds like the little gadget that people point at the car and it yelps like a kicked coyote."

"Coyote. Got it."

"Panic button, I'm not sure. It says if you don't get it fixed you may find yourself permanently locked out of the car."

"I hate when that happens."

She sat in the galley and read the letter, looked at the postmark. "This is from the dealer, in Santa Barbara. Somehow they found your right address."

"I'm picturing those guys locked out of all their drugs."

"Don't worry. They'd take a can opener to it."

I said "Maybe we should go up there."

"To Santa Barbara?"

"Yeah."

"Drive?"

"No. Take the boat. Ted is still shrimping out of Santa Barbara Marina, and now his son has a boat, too. We could probably get them to find us space at the commercial dock."

We had met Ted and his wife Debbie at the Wednesday morning street market in Santa Monica, where they sold the ridgeback shrimp and spot prawns they caught in their trawl nets. We became friends, and had taken *Den Mother* from time to time to visit them in Santa Barbara. Without their help you would have to commit murder to find a transient slip for a forty-eight foot boat in the tiny Santa Barbara Marina. Actually, one murder might not be enough. There's a waiting list for slips there that goes on for several generations; people get put on the list when they're born.

Maria said "They won't be able to fix your panic button if you don't have the car."

"Good point. But I don't know where it is. And I need to get out of here. All I can think about is what would happen to me if that car turns up with drugs in it, or even just with my fingerprints in it. They'd never get all the traces of dope out. The dogs would still be able to tell."

She smiled. "I know. They've got those cute little beagles. I saw them at the airport when we came back from Paris."

"How come I'm thinking about going to prison for twenty years, and you're thinking about cute little beagles?"

She didn't answer, and I saw that she was staring out the hatch at something across the channel. The docks on the far side were being rebuilt, and were empty of boats. To discourage sea birds from fouling the unoccupied docks the owner had strung a network of twine overhead, and a seagull had become ensnared in it, dangling by one wing. It was flapping the other wing helplessly. From the slow determined way the bird was moving its free wing I had the sense it had been hanging there a long time.

Maria said "Jesus."

I have always been particularly fond of birds. I took a pair of wire cutters from my toolbox, got into the dinghy, and rowed across the channel until my little boat floated directly underneath the unlucky creature. I spoke to it, saying "You stupid bird, what a mess you've got yourself into," then clipped it loose on both sides of the loop it had managed to make around its wing. The seagull shook its feathers and paddled around for a moment, with a pouty 'what the hell was that all about?' look, then flew a short distance, settling back into the water. Its wing was damaged. I wasn't doing so well either.

Maria watched from the salon hatch as I rowed back across the channel and tied up the boat. When I got back aboard she said "You know, in many cultures gods or spirits often manifest themselves to people in the form of animals."

"UCLA, undergraduate course in Eastern religions?"

"No. Mexican tradition has many stories of spirits appearing to people as birds or animals."

"You mean, like the myth of Leda and the Swan?"

"Well, that's Greek, and it's not the one I would have chosen."

"I can understand that, from a woman's perspective. I'm sure Leda didn't enjoy having sex with a swan."

She made a face. "Would you?"

How had we gotten here?

"Anyway, I said, "if that seagull was a spirit, I'm in trouble."

"Why?"

"I called it stupid."

"Maybe so, but you did him a favor."

I thought it over. Much as I could have used divine intervention, I thought I knew who the seagull represented.

45

*   *   *

Later, I stood in the galley dismembering the chicken Maria had brought home from the Friday street market. Though not technically free rangers, Chicken Man told us that his birds led fulfilled lives. In fact, they were the best you could buy locally, and had cured us of all supermarket chickens.

Many people believe that chickens occur in convenient ready-to-cook pieces, but this is not the case. There is some disassembly required. This was my fifth or sixth attempt at reducing a chicken to its parts, and the results were starting to look more like food and less like the work of wild dogs.

"Kind of ironic, though, isn't it?" I said. "Free the first bird, hack up the second. All in the same afternoon."

Maria said "I see that. To be consistent you should have eaten the seagull."

"I don't think I want to be consistent that badly. If I ever eat a seagull it'll be on a desert island."

"I just hope I'm not there with you."

"I would need you there."

"For sex."

"Of course."

The slightly banged-up chicken parts were sauteed in a pan with vermouth and little French olives called picholines. She presented it with a salad of buffalo mozzarella and tomato slices, garnished with my costly Cosa Nostra balsamic vinegar and olive oil. Maria opened a bottle of white Bordeaux and poured herself a glass.

She said "I saw a recipe for baked crows, once. In Spanish. It began '*Cuando creas que sea necesario comer cuevo...*' If you ever find it necessary to eat crows..."

"Sounds awfully tough."

"That's the problem. You blanche them first, in boiling water." She took a sip of wine. "Oh, that reminds me, the MasterCard people called again last night."

"Again?"

"You were asleep both times. The first time I answered in Spanish because I was sure it was my mother, then I told him I couldn't speak English."

"You did your Cisco Kid routine?"

"It got him off the line, but last night they called back with a Spanish speaker."

"Clever."

"Maybe. I told him to fuck his grandmother."

"You didn't."

"He said they had canceled the credit card."

"They think of everything. Did he say that before or after the part about his grandmother?"

"Before."

We ate our dinner, listening to the wind push little whitecaps down C Basin and slap them against the hull.

I said "You think Gizzi and Cannizzarro did this to me?"

"Why are you asking me? Go over there and ask them."

I said "I think I'll wait until the next class."

"Back to being a big lump of Playgo?"

"Play-doh. No, that's not it. I've paid for five more cooking classes. I want my money's worth."

10

D *en Mother* was about seventeen miles out of Marina del Rey on a heading of 240 degrees magnetic, which put us just off Point Dume. Right around the corner was Zuma Beach, which we would see presently. The autopilot was engaged, and I was sitting at the helm drinking coffee and reading the newspaper. I had a kitchen timer, and every ten minutes I checked the engine temperature on both sides and the oil pressure. Piece of cake.

Maria had undertaken the responsibility of seeing to it that we didn't hit anything. There was a tentative early morning breeze and a low, gentle swell. Light haze. Ideal powerboat conditions.

My approach to boating is to get out on the ocean at dawn, spend no more than five or six hours under way, and get back into protected water around lunchtime, avoiding the afternoon wind and chop. If it's blowing in the morning we stay put and have a big breakfast.

True, I will never write a thrilling account of courage and survival on board a small boat in the middle of some ocean, but it doesn't bother me. I find ordinary day-to-day existence plenty daunting enough, and I would like to keep the concept of pleasure in the activity known as pleasure boating. When everyone on board is vomiting, heavy objects are flying around below decks and survival seems questionable, it is not a pleasure. It is the opposite of pleasure.

Right now, just off to starboard were the high palisades of Point Dume, home of rock stars, actors and assorted moguls.

Maria pointed to the shoreline at the base of the cliffs. "Isn't that where the nude beach used to be?"

It's a staple of LA culture that people will find a secluded corner of beach somewhere and go naked. This lasts until the place becomes popular, maybe a month or two, at which point policemen will appear and insist that bathing suits be worn. After a couple of weekends of this, arrests are made. The signal that the fun will soon be over is the appearance on the beach of Japanese tourists in suits, bearing videocams. When they start to show up, the end is a week or two away. A couple of years later, the whole thing will start over.

I said "I always used to wonder what the State Bar would do to me if I was arrested on that beach."

"Spank you?"

"A competent self-respecting attorney would not disrobe on the beach."

"It reflects poorly on the profession?"

"Exactly."

"Exposes its shortcomings to the world?"

"Was that a dick joke? You're starting to sound like me."

She said something under her breath, but it was lost beneath the roar of *Den Mother*'s twin Chryslers.

Many years of standup comedy workshops, improv, and

open mike performances at local comedy venues, had left me with little resistance to a decent set-up, or an indecent set-up, regardless of the circumstances. It's a dangerous condition, particularly for a lawyer, and it can be communicable.

From her seat next to me at the control station Maria looked down into the salon, then went down the ladder and returned with a squealing cell phone.

I said "You've got good ears."

"I thought you turned this off before we left."

"The only people who know the number are you and the office." But it wasn't so.

"Larry, how'd you get this number?"

"Never mind. I have to see you right away. Where are you?"

"In Court, downtown."

"What's that noise?"

"I don't hear anything."

"You're in the Federal Building? Come upstairs and see me."

"I'm in Superior Court, and I'm working. The clerk is going to call my case any minute."

"Let me come down to the boat tonight, ok?"

"Fine. Make it after eight."

"Gotta deal."

Maria looked at me. "After eight, what?"

I turned off the phone. "After eight Larry Hayden discovers something about living on board that he hadn't anticipated."

"He'll be pissed."

"I'm pissed. Nobody knows this number."

"Not any more."

We had rounded Point Dume and were passing Zuma Beach, then Trancas. Thirteen knots at three thousand rpm, engine temp and oil pressure steady on both sides. No funny noises. Ahead would be Point Mugu, Port Hueneme and finally Ventura Marina, anticipated time of arrival one o'clock.

Tomorrow, Santa Barbara.

Maria said "We're going to Santa Barbara to avoid Larry Hayden?"

"I like to take the boat there. You like it there. Ted's made space for us at the commercial dock. We can get fresh ridgebacks and spot prawns right on the pier. You like to walk on State Street."

"And..."

"I have a sense that something bad may be coming and I didn't feel like waiting there at the dock in Marina del Rey until it catches up with me. And the Lincoln-Mercury dealer is the only lead we've got. They must have some paperwork on the Lincoln. And I don't know what else to do."

She picked up the newspaper I'd been reading. "Maybe this is why your buddy Larry wants to see you."

"What?"

"Mob boss murdered," she read. "It says they found him shot five times, under a bulldozer."

"They probably shot him first."

"What do you mean?"

"You ever try to shoot someone under a bulldozer?"

"Maybe he was hiding."

"Let me guess. Was his name Aragosta?"

"Cozzi."

"His nickname wasn't 'the Lobster,' or something like that, was it?"

"Yeah. It says it right here. The lobster." She gave me a look. "How many Mafia bosses do you know?"

"Only the ones who do the cooking classes."

51

11

M ost people would probably want to live in Santa Barbara if they knew it was there. If you decided to move to Southern California you might start with Los Angeles. It has name recognition. After a few years you will begin to take the palm trees and mild weather for granted. You will get tired of driving on freeways. You will forget the thrill of living in a big city because you'll begin to notice you're not actually living in one anymore. Now you're ready for Santa Barbara, an unnaturally pretty town.

Den Mother rested in a slot at the commercial dock. Ted had helped us to back in to the stern-to docking arrangement used by the fishing boats. We had taken the tram from the waterfront as far as it went up State Street, then walked a few blocks to Santa Barbara Lincoln Mercury, a newly constructed but architecturally correct structure in Spanish Mission style, with a facade of high imposing arches heavily embellished with cake-frosting squiggles in cast concrete. Through the broad windows could be seen various glittering vehicles; brass rings on the merry-go-round of the American experience.

In any other town I would have worried about my blue jeans, my tee shirt, and Maria's fetching but casual cut-offs and yellow macramé halter top. But in Santa Barbara only servants need uniforms. The rich dress like beach bums. It drives foreigners crazy.

On entering the showroom we were approached by a worried-looking middle-aged man in a sturdy Sears Roebuck suit. A gin drinker, by his complexion. The first white person I had seen in Santa Barbara without a suntan. Thinning grey hair that went well with the gray polyester overtones of the suit. On his breast pocket was a nametag that indicated he was Morris Tupper, and I realized the entire visit was going to be a struggle to keep away from this compelling setup. Tupperware, Tupperware, the word rang in my head. A good punch line is like intestinal gas; the compulsion to let it out is irresistible.

"A Lincoln Navigator," said Mr. Tupper, "yes. We have seven on the lot, yes."

Up close, the car of my nightmares was much bigger than I remembered. As Mr. Tupper listed its virtues he kept using the word 'upscale.' Power-deployable running boards were upscale. You opened the passenger doors and the running boards slid out, obedient servants for those unwilling or unable to lift a leg high enough to mount the beast. With the touch of a button the back seats curled up like snails, the back hatch went up, went down. Upscale. Tell it where you want to go and a canned voice gives directions; 'turn right at the next corner.' Fifty grand takes you where you want to go.

I showed Mr. Tupper the recall notice and said "Remember me? I bought one of these from you last summer."

He furrowed his brow. "You did? I sell one or two Navigators a week, but I remember my customers."

54

"I was wearing a suit."

"Ah."

"And my hair was different. Shorter." I gestured toward Maria. "And my wife was not with me."

She smiled graciously.

Mr. Tupper had given up trying to remember us and was reading the recall notice.

"If your car is here we can fix the keyless entry control. Leave it overnight. We'll give you a loaner."

I said "It was stolen. Actually, I thought I'd get a copy of your file. Help me complete the insurance forms."

This clever ruse had occurred to me at *Den Mother's* helm, during the passage from Ventura Marina to Santa Barbara that morning. The risk was that the MasterCard people had already been here, which would make me look like the crook who had bought the car with a fake credit card in the first place. In this scenario the Lincoln dealer then calls the police and I get arrested with a story that would take weeks to sort out. This bad outcome did not take place, although another one did.

Mr. Tupper pointed me toward a corner office in which a lady who bore a remarkable resemblance to Margaret Dumont explained to me that Santa Barbara Lincoln Mercury was a 'paperless' operation. She then looked for the transaction in her computer, found it, and ordered the machine to print a copy of everything, which it did. She gave me the copies.

"No charge," she said, then looked up over my shoulder. Before I could turn around to see what had caught her eye I was grabbed hard by the upper arms by two men, one of whom said "Shaddup,' which made no sense since I had not said anything. I was dragged backwards across the showroom floor into the backseat of a Lincoln Town Car. One of the men got into the drivers seat. The other sat beside me. I had expected a heavy, but he had a salesman's affable look, sandy hair, blue and white seersucker jacket and red-white-and-blue striped rep tie. Patriotic. Mid-forties. I pictured him in a straw boater and campaign buttons. 'I Like Ike.' He looked more tired than angry. He held a little nickel-plated semi-automatic pistol, probably a .380.

"Mr. McGuire," he said, "you shouldn't have come here."

"It's starting to look that way," I said.

The car started and we began to move out toward the street. My captor looked toward the man in the front seat. "Arnie," he said, "What we're going to have to do here is –"

He was interrupted by the sound of screeching brakes followed by the crunch and sound of breaking glass of a moderate impact. We had been hit. Inside the car an airbag inflated with a sound like a gunshot, pinning Arnie in place and scaring the hell out of the rest of us. Then the sound of another collision. Not us, this time, but nearby, accompanied by a rising chorus of voices, some yelling.

From the backseat window I could see a red Lincoln Navigator parked in a traffic lane right in front of the showroom. Maria was standing on its hood, waving her yellow macrame halter at the traffic. She had set loose her puppies. This distraction had no doubt caused the two collisions. Traffic was now completely blocked in both directions and there was a growing crowd of pedestrians on both sides of the street. I heard the sound of approaching sirens. Seersucker jacket was staring out the backseat window. The .380 was still in his hand but no longer pointed at me. I turned sideways on the seat and kicked his wrist, sending the pistol flying off somewhere into the depths of Lincolnland. At this moment Arnie emerged from the collapsing billows of the airbag. He had a nosebleed and a dazed expression. He looked at his pal. Then the two of them stared at Maria in full Joan of Arc mode, waving from the hood of the Navigator at the gathering crowd. You'd think neither of them had ever seen a bare-breasted woman before. Evidently, whatever they had planned for me no longer seemed like a good idea because they both bailed out of the rather grand Lincoln Town Car and walked off into the crowd.

I got out and waved at Maria, calling her name. She

jumped down off her perch, fastening her halter at the same time, an exercise that could have got her a job at the Cirque de Soliel. Together, we walked back through the showroom to the back lot, then out onto a side street, away from the growing sounds of commotion.

On the next corner we found a shop catering to tourists, in which I bought a pair of mirror shades and a blue gimme cap bearing the legend 'Santa Barbara Dreamin.' Maria bought a straw hat and a demure terrycloth warm-up jacket with pictures of sailboats on it.

Transformed by our new apparel, we found a promising Italian restaurant in an inner courtyard of a shopping block, with tables arranged around a fountain. Grape hyacinth hung from the eaves all around, mixing its scent with the moist air and music of falling water from the fountain.

We had some nice cold Pinot Grigio, then a seafood salad.

Maria said "Mr. Tuttle was showing me another Lincoln Navigator. Next year's model. Then I saw those guys grab you. I was sitting in the front seat of the Navigator and he was showing me how the automatic something worked, I forget what, but the engine had to be running or it wouldn't work."

"Tupper."

"What?"

"His name was Tupper, not Tuttle."

"Whatever. You want to hear this story or don't you?"

"Never mind."

"Anyway, whatshisface tried to make a move when he saw what was happening to you, but I locked him out of the car. Then I put it in gear and drove the thing out onto the street, I thought maybe I would find a cop, but then I remembered what we were talking about on the way up, about the nude beach-"

"-It's an intelligence test."

"What is?"

"There's a kind of intelligence test where they put you in

a room with a weird assortment of materials and ask you to solve some kind of a problem. In order to figure it out, you have to use familiar materials in unaccustomed ways."

She sipped her Pinot Grigio, then looked down at her chest. "So my chest is a familiar material?"

"To some lucky people."

"We've got to go back on the street sooner or later. What if I get arrested?"

"For indecent exposure?"

"I guess."

I ordered another glass of wine. "Ok, so somebody says there was a bare-breasted woman standing on a car waiving her bra. Nobody at the Lincoln place is going to admit to knowing anything about it, so the cops go out and round up all the bare-breasted women they can find and put them in a lineup, right?"

She made a face. "It's not funny."

"Then, 'cause all the witnesses are men, and all they saw were the breasts, it becomes a process of identifying the breasts, like 'I think number four looks like them, but they were higher and more pointed'."

"Stop it. You wouldn't think it was so funny if you had breasts."

"My friends would."

58

12

I do not like to go boating at night but it didn't feel right to remain in the Santa Barbara Marina after the events at the Lincoln Mercury showroom. And I had what I had gone there to get; copies of the sale documents for the 'other' Tom McGuire's purchase of a Lincoln Navigator, forgotten by Arnie and his patriotic pal in the ensuing fracas.

We were back out on the ocean. There was a three-quarter moon, almost like daylight once you got used to it. The lights of Santa Barbara had disappeared in the evening mist. Wind and waves coming from behind us; oil drilling platforms looming to starboard. It was going to be downhill all the way to Ventura Marina.

I said "He lives in Boyle Heights."

Maria said "Who does?"

"Thomas McGuire. The one who bought the car."

"So you're going to pay him a visit?"

"Don't see as I have any choice."

"It's probably just some kind of a mail drop."

"Most likely."

"But it might be dangerous."

"Yes."

I thought about it for a moment.

"Dangerous. You think I'm an incompetent bumbler?"

"I didn't say that. These people are serious. They have guns."

"Well, after we got hit and the airbag inflated, I kicked the gun out of the guy's hand. I thought I was doing alright."

"That was after I took off my top and made the cars crash." She paused. "I flash my boobies to get you out of a jam and then at lunch you're giving me titty jokes."

"Hurt your feelings?"

"No. My feelings are fine. Are you sure you're ready for more of this stuff?"

"You mean am I prepared to go to Boyle Heights without your bare breasts to protect me?"

She giggled. "That's not exactly what I meant."

"I'm sure I can think up other ways to cause a commotion. If you're not around I'll drop my pants."

A perfect setup for another dick joke; I can't help myself. She either didn't notice or was being nice about it.

It was too bad I had lost track of that nickel-plated .380.

*   *   *

The Boyle Heights address turned out to be Mendoza's Modern Car Wash. Did I want to get my car washed? The car I was driving wasn't even mine; an old Volvo with Gore-Lieberman stickers on the back bumper. I did legal work for a used car dealer who paid me in used cars. When one of them broke down, or I got bored with it, I would drive over to the lot and pick out another one.

I paid seven dollars to wash the Volvo. I was offered coffee and cookies, but declined. Behind the car wash I could see a two-story stucco bungalow. I approached it with caution. The ground floor windows were boarded up. A dead palm tree stood in the fenced yard, which was barren of grass but liberally dotted with dog droppings. I stood at the open gate, looking and listening for the source of the doggie poo. Nothing. Maybe the stuff had been put there by someone who wanted to discourage burglars but couldn't afford a dog.

In the entryway were four mailboxes, one of which was marked 'McGuire/Mendoza. I stood and stared at it, mildly stupified.

I should have looked around to see if anyone was watching, then reached into the mailbox and stolen the mail, but I did it backwards; steal first, then look. Too bad for me. When I did look up there was someone in a parked car out on the street who appeared to be taking my picture through a telephoto lens. Too late now. I stuffed the letters in my pocket and walked back through the car wash to the street, where a well-dressed, overweight man sat behind the wheel of a beige Chevrolet. He had a dark moustache, a middle-eastern appearance. He had put away the camera, but I thought I could see some kind of a large handgun next to him on the front seat, partly covered by a newspaper.

I said "Can I help you," which as we all know is code for 'who the fuck are you and/or what are you doing here?'

He smiled, and extended his hand through the driver's side window, and said "Amir Mahmoud." I told him my name. We shook hands. He acted as if he knew me. Then I remembered Mr. Mahmoud, the MasterCard fraud investigator.

I gestured toward the passenger side of the front seat. "Is that what I think it is?"

He frowned and adjusted the newspaper so that it covered his weapon. Then he smiled. "Afghanistan," he said, as though it explained something. "Don't worry, I am fully licensed."

I was not worried about being shot by Mr. Mahmoud, with or without a license. I had about two seconds to contemplate the impossibility of explaining anything to this guy, when we were distracted by a commotion in the car wash; shouts, curses. Some kids on the sidewalk were laughing and pointing at my car, which was advancing slowly through the wash cycle with all four windows down.

13

At Frankenstein's Quality Cars, my client Al Frankenstein stood proudly amid his herd of clunkers, the wind whipping through a thousand little plastic flags strung overhead. He thought the car wash story was funny.

"You're supposed to close the windows before they wash the car," he said. I agreed with him that this was so. "I woulda figured a smart guy like you to know things like that."

They don't miss a chance to humiliate or belittle the lawyer. Getting even, I suppose. The soggy state of the Volvo did not faze him.

"Water's nothing. You get a car somebody died in, maybe no one found the body for a few days, now you got a real problem. Nobody's gonna buy a smelly car."

"I promise I won't do that, ok?"

Al was a short, muscular middle-aged man with gray curly hair and dark fiery eyes, jammed into a bullet-proof pinstripe suit. He looked like he was about to overthrow the Government. If he told you to buy one of his cars, you bought it. I'd watched him work; it was awesome.

"Naw," he said. "You're the best, Tom. You wanna die in one of my cars, be my guest."

I checked him for a smile; didn't see one. After wandering around on the lot for a few minutes I found a red mid-90's Eldorado convertible and drove it back to the Marina.

*   *   *

The stolen mail situation was not so easily mended. What I had taken from the mailbox marked McGuire/ Mendoza were three new credit cards issued to Thomas McGuire. No big deal if they were never used. Evidence, I thought. But evidence of what? How many more of these things were out there, and where were they coming from? I didn't think I was going to be able to go back to Mendoza's Car Wash to retrieve any more mail. I thought briefly about filing a change of address with the Post Office, then realized my mind was going adrift.

At the office I photocopied the new credit cards and the printed materials that came with them. Then, taking my cue from Al Frankenstein I wrote 'deceased - return to sender' on each envelope and dropped them in the mail.

Mr. Mahmoud was another matter. His photographs were entirely plausible evidence that I was a crook. Visions of mail fraud danced in my head.

I looked out my office window at the Marina, and the thin band of ocean visible beyond the shoreline apartments. Every year they built more buildings in Marina del Rey, traffic got worse, and little by little the marine environment disappeared behind concrete and masonry. Now there was a design control board; every building, sign, fence, must reflect a nautical motif. Obviously, the beginning of the end; what the late radio personality Jean Shepherd, god of my adolescence, called 'creeping meatballism.'

I looked down at the street, doing my automatic check for Lincoln Navigators; spotting a white one northbound on Admiralty Way. Impossible to eyeball the driver at this angle. Maria said I was having a panic reaction whenever I saw one, so I had a chat with the psychiatrist down the hall from my office. When I finished telling him the story he stared at me as if I had mackerel coming out of my ears. He wrote me a prescription for Xanax and told me to call the police. I didn't take the advice but I tried taking the pills. They put me to sleep. At the time, I thought this was a disadvantage. Since all this craziness had started I was putting in longer hours at the office. I felt safe there.

When I left the office Southern California was winding up the late November day with a warm summer evening, complete with a spectacular red and gold sunset over the ocean. Yeah, I know, it's what we get out here instead of culture. If it bothers you, go back East and freeze your buns off. I parked my new Eldo on the seawall. We had planned an early dinner. I had cooking class.

*   *   *

Victor Cannizzarro was explaining *Crostata Alla Marmellata* to a capacity crowd. The young hoodlums were not out tonight, but their absence was more than overcome by a great influx of Brentwood Ladies, and a few more guys. There were more than forty people where there had been twenty or so the last time. And there was a mood of breathless anticipation; something I hadn't noticed before. I suppose there wasn't much excitement in Brentwood since OJ left town. Tonight, jam tart. Film at eleven.

"You gotta know how to mix it up," Vic was saying, breaking an egg into a large mound of flour, sugar, butter and grated lemon rind. "Italians, they know what's what; the rest of

67

you gotta look sharp." A few knowing giggles, then the squeal of a cell phone. This lapse of taste has become the social equivalent of breaking wind in public, and disapproving glances were cast here and there in the crowd. But it was Cannizzarro who pulled a phone from his pocket and answered. He was looking down into his Crostata in progress, but after a few seconds he looked up sharply into the audience, then closed up the little clamshell telephone and put it away.

He gestured to a man in the second row. "You," he said, "c'mere a minute." They walked together toward the front of the store, then out of sight. There was a sense of foreboding. A few minutes later Vic came back alone, and resumed his station at the counter. "Just a little misunderstandin," he said, stirring the egg into the flour mixture a little too vigorously. He went on to roll out the dough, heat the marmalade and triple sec, but the mood had changed.

When the *Crostata Alla Marmellata* was ready to bake, two trays of fully-baked ones emerged from the oven. We were served small pieces of marmalade tart while Vic went on to *Cassata Alla Siciliana*, which turned out to be pound cake with sweetened ricotta cheese and chocolate. Brentwood Ladies would spend time in Purgatory for this one, or at least on a Stairmaster.

I wasn't much interested in desserts, so I decided I would take a break and get some air. As I was leaving, Vic was melting chocolate, butter and espresso in a *bain Marie.*

As I stood on the sidewalk outside the store someone called my name, and I crossed the street to find Larry Hayden sitting in an unmarked motor pool sedan with the ousted would-be cooking student, a youngish blond man with a wispy little moustache, a standard blue suit and brutal haircut. This one actually got out of the car and opened the back door for me, which I thought was very courteous.

I nodded to my former classmate. "You're with the Bureau, I guess." He looked at Larry for permission, then agreed. "Won't all the other Agents laugh when they find out you were thrown out of cooking school?"

They made dour faces. Not funny.

Larry said "What were they doing in there?"

"Cooking, Larry. Same as last time you asked. It's a cooking demonstration. We were making a marmalade tart, then some kind of heavy-duty Sicilian pound cake."

"There's O.C. guys in there, Tom."

"Well, it's not a secret." I gestured across the street to the storefront, where the legend 'La Cosa Nostra' appeared in blue neon.

"Cannizzarro made Jerome, here," Larry said. "How'd he do that?"

"He got a phone call."

"You're consorting with known criminals. You want to be careful."

I said, "Be reasonable. I'm not on probation; I can consort all I want. Anyway, I'm not consorting, I'm taking cooking classes. There's about forty people in there right now. You want to bring up a paddy wagon, take them downtown and book them for conspiracy to make pound cake?"

Jerome snickered. Larry glared at him. I had the impression Jerome did not see infiltrating a cooking class to be a career-enhancing assignment, particularly since he had failed at it so miserably.

We passed a few more minutes in this way. Larry asked about my practice; declined to tell me about the cases currently being worked on in his office, complained about the scheduled pay raise the President had nixed. Same old stuff. Then the class let out and Brentwood Ladies started leaving the store in small clumps, talking, one would assume, about *crostata*, the Mafia and the disappearance of the man in the second row. A few of them glanced in our direction.

I made my goodbyes to Larry and Jerome and went back into the store, where I found Vic Cannizzarro by himself, stacking folding chairs and whistling a theme from *The Barber of Seville*.

69

I said "The classes have been fun. You noticed I've been there?"

He didn't look at me, continued stacking chairs. "Yeah. Lou thinks it's funny, you coming to our cooking classes. Me, I dunno what's on your mind. Feds sent a stooge in here tonight, I hadda boot him out. Scumbag probably had a wire." He scowled. "And they park across the street, like I'm gonna get scared and cancel the class." He paused. "Y'know what I did?" He looked around at me and stopped stacking chairs. "I told em all about it tonight, all the customers. I said 'you know how authentic this class is? We got Government ringers; I just trew one out, and look when you leave tonight, they're parked across the street tryin a see what we're doing.'"

"You'll scare away your students."

He snorted. "That's what you think. They love it. They're standin' up for their rights, the way they see it, like the demonstrations they went to years ago, when they were kids."

"Sort of like 'hey, hey, LBJ, how many tarts did you bake today?'"

He squinted at me. He said "What the fuck are you talking about?" and started stacking folding chairs again, banging them together loudly.

"Did Lou tell you I came by here looking for an SUV, a Lincoln Navigator?"

"Maybe."

"He told me to look for the car down south of here and I went down there and got up to my ass in trouble."

"Not my trouble."

"Lou sent me down there."

He took off his chef's garb, revealing a truly remarkable black cashmere suit, a little too warm for LA but formidable as hell. "Hey McGuire," he said, "get outta my face. You got a problem with Lou, you ask him. I told him, was upta me you wouldn't even be in the classes, the kinda friends you got. So say goodnight, ok?"

I said goodnight.

70

14

I had to stand in line at the Post Office for the letter because it was registered, return receipt, and could not have been left in my box at the Marina. It was from MasterCard, covered with seals and stamps. All it needed was a skull-and-crossbones.

I held it up to show Maria, who was below in the galley, chopping fresh spices for chicken coconut soup.

She said "Don't open it." Just like last time.

"I know, ancient Hispanic advice, but I signed for it. Anyway I already opened it."

"And?"

"It's from Mr. Mahmoud, the MasterCard fraud guy. He says if I return the Lincoln to them in good shape they may decide not to prosecute me for mail fraud."

"You told me once that when you threaten to take someone to the authorities to get an advantage in a dispute you're having with him, it's extortion."

"Yeah, it is."

"And that's a crime, right?"

"It's a crime when you or I do it, but not when banks and insurance companies do it."

"What are you talking about?"

"At least not during a Republican administration."

She resumed chopping up a thick stalk of lemon grass, then some galanga root. "Try to have a serious conversation with you..."

"Oh, it's serious enough. I've got to get the car back. Can you hear me trying to explain why I was taking mail addressed to me out of a mailbox behind a carwash in Boyle Heights?"

She thought for a moment. "You could try, but it would sound stupid and nobody would believe you."

"Right. Mahmoud's boys would nail me, but now they want to make nice instead. Just give back their car and they'll forget the rest."

"And give you your credit card back?"

"Probably not."

"So go over to Brentwood and ask your pals to help you find the car. It worked once, kind of. Try not to buy too much fancy food while you're over there."

It was a logical idea; give back the Lincoln and it's a walkaway. But I had developed a sense by then that the Lincoln was chasing me. The idea of me chasing the Lincoln didn't appeal. It was what had gotten me into trouble in the first place.

I took out the folder of papers Margaret Dumont had given me at the Lincoln showroom in Santa Barbara and spread them out in the salon, which was at that moment fragrant with the aroma of coconut milk in chicken stock.

There was a copy of the luxurious folio-sized Navigator brochure, slickly printed on heavy stock. It was as I remembered from Santa Barbara. The bumpers went up and down like little elevators in case owners were too fat or weighted down with jewelry to make the leap up into the passenger compartment. Rear seats would curl up on command, obedient self-effacing snails, leaving more room aft for the cord of wood or herd of cattle or whatever else you might be schlepping around the neighborhood. The GPS system took the place of maps. Just tell it where you want to go, and it would provide driving instructions, in English, though it could be jiggered around to spout French, German, Italian and a few other languages. There was a strong suggestion that the Lincoln Navigator was more than a machine providing transportation. It was an icon; and not merely a symbol of something transcendent, but an embodiment. An entire page of the brochure consisted of a close-up shot of a bowl of mashed potatoes. What was the meaning of this?

There were anti-theft systems; it would howl like a motherless child if someone other than its owners attempted to get inside. And if some clap-stricken moke managed to drive it off, there was LoJack, not standard equipment, but as an option.

"LoJack," I said.

Maria had the exhaust fan on in the galley, and couldn't hear me.

"LoJack."

This time she looked up.

I said "Do you know what that is?"

"A card game?"

"It finds your car when it's stolen."

"How does it do that?"

"Think of it as a little special-purpose cell phone. It takes power off the car's battery. Mostly, it stays turned off, but when you call the company and tell them the car's been stolen, they send out a signal that turns the gadget on and it tells them where the car is located."

Maria said "They put those in small children now."

"What?"

"Sure. Kid doesn't turn up for dinner, you call the control tower and they tell you he's down at the pool hall smoking dope with his friends."

"Small children smoke dope in pool halls?"

She said "Where've you been?" then smiled.

"You had me there for a minute."

"Give it a few years. You want to bet me it won't happen?"

I thought about it for a moment. "No, I'll pass on the bet, but forget the pool halls. They smoke dope at video arcades now. Maybe your brothers smoked dope in pool halls."

"Leave my brothers out of this." She was finishing up the chicken galanga soup with makrut leaves and enough Sriraccha hot sauce to remove fillings from the teeth of the uninitiated. "You think," she said, "you could use this LoJack business to find the Lincoln?"

"If there is one installed on the car, then yeah. I'm afraid so."

15

Back to Brentwood. The morning was cold by LA standards. I put the top down on the Eldo and turned the radio and the heater way up. Someone had set the radio on an oldies station, and Little Richard doing *Lucille* did a lot to restore my spirits as I drove up San Vicente from the beach. The thing I couldn't figure was what exactly Lou Gizzi had done to me in Tijuana. Leaving the Lincoln unlocked with the keys in it, someone must have known I was coming. But anyone could have driven it away. Maybe the plan was for someone else to do it. But the gardener in San Diego was certainly a setup; waiting there for us with further instructions, like the kind of game kids played at camp; go to one place, find a clue, go on to the next one.

There was no action on the street when I parked; a

couple of trucks making deliveries, two sweepers. The blue neon letters that spelled out 'La Cosa Nostra' were dark. Inside, I found Lou Gizzi stacking boxes of arborio rice into a pyramid on a marble counter.

I said "It gets too soggy for dinner at eight."

Lou said "Huh?"

He turned towards me and squinted. He put down the box of rice he was holding. I wondered what Vic Cannizzarro had told him about our discussion after the last class. I wondered about his capacity for violence.

"My arborio?" He said. "It gets soggy?"

"Maria says so. Maybe you should get another brand."

"Nah. Vic's doing risotto classes next month. Let him figure it out."

"How can you spend a whole evening teaching people how to make a pot of rice, for Chrissake?"

He shrugged. "Ask Vic. He says over in Italy there's people spend their whole lives making that shit and they never get it right."

"Oh." I paused for a moment, collecting myself. "Listen, you remember the Lincoln Navigator?"

"Yeah. The one we found for you."

"Right." I told him the whole story, from San Diego to Tijuana to the fast food restaurant and the red rubber boys. I left out Mendoza's Modern Car Wash and Mr. Mahmoud's photos of me stealing the mail.

After a moment he said "Holy shit" in a neutral tone of voice. "So all this time, you've been figuring me for it?" He snorted. "You've been thinking I'm a drug smuggler and I'm dumb enough to get you to help me out?"

I decided to ignore the slur; nobody seemed to think I was smart enough to smuggle drugs. "You told me where to look for the Lincoln and I find it in one day, sitting there with the key in the ignition, all loaded and ready to go. It had to be a setup."

"Look, assuming just for the sake of argument I was

gonna commit a major felony at my age, you're the last person I'd want for help."

"Everyone keeps telling me that."

Two well dressed ladies walked into the store and began an animated conversation with Gizzi on the subject of truffle slicers, which La Cosa Nostra offered in three different models. Shortly, a handsome chrome-plated gadget was purchased and carried off with evident satisfaction. Truffle slicers at ten in the morning. What a life.

I said "I need some questions answered." I could see Lou making up his mind whether to go to street mode and tell me to blow it out my ass; deciding against it.

"So ask them," he said.

"You made a call to find the car, right?"

"I told ya."

"Whoever you talked to, you told him about me?"

Lou thought for a moment, picked up a box of arborio from the stack he had been making. "Maybe I made a mistake. What I did, I told this guy it was my friend's credit card and my friend was pissed. Maybe he thought you were a wiseguy. I never figured the cocksucker would take advantage."

"Maybe now that the fun is over you could ask him if I could just get the car back, he can keep the drugs?"

"Can't do it. He's dead."

"Wait a minute, is it the guy under the bulldozer, the one they called The Lobster?"

"Fuck you know about that?" He put both hands palm down on the marble counter. I had startled him.

I said "It was in the newspaper. Cossi; nickname The Lobster. They shot him five times, right?"

"Yeah, Cossi." He relaxed a little.

"What was that all about?"

"The bulldozer was stolen."

"People steal bulldozers?"

"Fuck yes. You start it up and drive it away. Like a car. You have any idea what they cost?"

"They killed him for stealing a bulldozer?"

"What do I know? The way I heard, it was a sideline. He would get his crew to steal big-ticket construction equipment, cranes, derricks, those giant corkscrews you see drill holes in the ground. People get pissed when they show up in the morning at a big project and some pile driver, five, six stories high, took a hike in the middle of the night."

"It must have annoyed a lot of people in the construction business."

"That's what I heard. Just rumors, y'unnerstand. But he was big. He should have known better. I heard he ran Santa Barbara; the seafood, legit businesses. Had a big place in Montecito, used to belong to some movie star. He liked to steal heavy equipment was all. Got a kick out of it."

"Lou, you know what a LoJack is?"

"Sure. Guy steals your car, you call the company, they tell the cops where it is. Cops get it back to you the same day. Got some bush-league guys in a lotta trouble before people caught on."

"You think maybe there's a LoJack on that Lincoln?"

He laughed. "That's how they found the bulldozer."

16

L   ate that afternoon I got a call at the office from Investigator
  Morse, the identity theft man I had come to think of as
Investigator Remorse since all he did was apologize for being
unable to help. Basically, he had nothing to report. I told him
about the possibility of a LoJack option on the Lincoln. He
called me back again within an hour.

"We know where your car is," he said.

"Not my car."

He made an exasperated noise. "You know, the Lincoln.
The Air Force has it. We're closing our file."

I turned to look out the window at the benign blue water
and ranks of boats in slips. 'Really?' was the best I could
manage.

"You know Mr. Mahmoud," he said, "with the anti-fraud

81

section at MasterCard?"

"Amir."

"Is that his name? He told me the Lincoln is at Vandenberg Air Force Base, up by Lompoc. He said he thought the Government was involved and we should close our file."

I considered explaining to Investigator Remorse how unlikely it would be for organized crime persons to have bought a Lincoln Navigator in my name on a fake credit card, and turned it over to the Air Force. But he seemed pleased with the story, and with the idea that he could close his file, so I figured I would make it easy. He was going to close the file no matter what I said and he wasn't going to do me any good one way or the other. Why struggle?

"Of course," I said. "With the Government involved, what would be the point of cluttering up your files with the matter?"

Encouraged, Investigator Remorse then ended the conversation, happy with the thought that the Lincoln, source of all my tribulation, was evidently destined to be shot into space or used to lead an invasion of some hapless Middle Eastern country, and that he could therefore close his file. Where do people get this faith in Government?

Then I got a call from Amir Mahmoud. He was huffy with me for not telling him the whole story. The vehicle did have the LoJack option, as I had suggested, and had been located by its telltale radio beacon on the premises of Vandenberg Air Force Base. At which point, Mr. Mahmoud said, he had written a registered letter to the Secretary of the Air Force, copy to the Commanding Officer at Vandenberg, describing the Lincoln Navigator and demanding its immediate return. He would figure out what to do with me later. I think he believed I was a spy, or some sort of secret agent.

That evening, on board *Den Mother*, I had to tell Maria the story three times before she would believe I wasn't making it up. It was kind of insulting, really. First, nobody would believe I was smart enough to smuggle drugs, now Maria thought the idea that I was a spy was laughable.

"Mahmoud doesn't think it's so funny," I said. "Neither does Investigator Morse."

"Tom, if you're a secret agent I'm a *tostada grande con queso.*"

"Make fun of me."

"Don't feel bad. It makes a great story and the MasterCard people are buying it."

"But it isn't going to last because it isn't so."

"That you're a spy?"

"No. Yes. I mean the Lincoln isn't at Vandenberg Air Force Base."

"It isn't?"

I had bought a US Geological Survey 7.5 minute quadrangle map on my way home, showing Vandenberg and the surrounding area. I unrolled it on the galley table.

"You see the area marked Vandenberg?'"

"They don't show any detail inside."

"Right. It's classified. But look up along the coast; you see the area that's a different color?"

"It says Point Sal Beach State Park."

"Right."

"It's completely surrounded by Vandenberg, except for the ocean. How'd the Air Force let them get away with putting the beach there?"

"It was a long time ago."

"And that's where the Lincoln is?"

"Gotta be. If I have to choose between Vandenberg and Point Sal Beach, it isn't even close. Vandenberg is a military base. Point Sal Beach is a hangout. Anything weird going on in the area, it'll be there."

She went to the channel-side salon hatch, opened it, and lit a cigarette. She hadn't smoked for years. I didn't know she had cigarettes on board. Silence, I thought, would be best at this point.

She pitched the cigarette, turned back from the darkness of C Basin. "You want me to believe someone has taken this

83

miserable car of yours to the beach?"

She started out in a trying-hard-to-be-logical tone, but her voice rose as she spoke. I said nothing. "They're hoodlums," she went on, "that's what that asshole friend of yours told you. So now they're at the beach. Do you suppose they brought sandwiches and cold drinks? A portable radio? Sunblock? I can see them up there, dancing on the sand."

"Why does this make you angry at me?"

She drew a long breath. "Because you are the dope of the universe. Because you want to go to this *pinche* beach of yours, you're so smart you know exactly where it is, and when you get there, what? What will you do to them?"

"What I had in mind was-"

"-No."

"No?"

"I'm not going with you this time."

But the next day I swapped the Eldo with Al Frankenstein for a dented, early-eighties Ford half-ton pickup with a camper shell, and we drove north. I guess Maria figured if she didn't come with me she might never see me again.

I could imagine them up there on the sand; dark, hairy crooks with pot bellies in voluminous Hawaiian-print bathing suits, dancing solemnly in a circle around the Lincoln Navigator. Maybe chanting something. I had started taking the Xanax again, had a bottle of it with me.

As we drove up US 1 I started working my way into avenging angel mode. We were penetrating to the heart of things and would soon see justice done. To Maria, I used the same proposal I had advanced to explain the trip to Tijuana; just checking things out, no engagement of the enemy. She clearly didn't believe me this time, if she ever had, but she must have realized there was no stopping me. This was what I had been waiting for.

17

We stopped at Oxnard and spoke to a Parks Department representative, a bored young lady with too much lipstick and a pierced eyelid. The phrase 'Point Sal Beach State Park' meant nothing to her, but she made a phone call, then told us we wouldn't be able to get there; the road was out. And there were no facilities, "not even toilets," which seemed to settle the matter as far as she was concerned. I told her that this country was settled by brave people who were willing to go where there were no toilets. She did not seem interested.

Maria said nothing. Sanitation facilities on board our camper were primitive, as were the beds and cooking arrangements. Maria had examined them with disdain and announced that she would have little to do with them, even with the beds, which would be used for strictly limited purposes, despite the bumper sticker someone had put on the back door of the camper shell, which lewdly announced 'If this camper's rockin' please don't be knockin.'

We continued north on US 1. After a while Maria said "The road is out, Tom. Did you hear her?"

"That just means the Parks Department doesn't want you to go there. Neither does the Air Force. Particularly since 9/11. It's right in their armpit."

"What do they do there?"

"Launch missiles."

"Oh."

"Years ago I represented a guy who grew oranges outside of Santa Maria. He took me to parties at Point Sal. They were saying the road was out back then. Big signs on the road that said 'danger - road washed out ahead.' Keeps out the tourists. When you see it, you'll know why. It's some of the last completely unspoiled coastline in Central California. Back then, the locals called it 'Paradise.' There were people who lived there during the summer, or they used to."

"Without toilets?"

"Without anything. In tents, lean-tos made of driftwood, a few shacks up on the bluff. You could dive for lobsters, you could fish. There were calico bass out in the kelp, big halibut just past the surf line, mussels on the rocks. Those were some parties. They would build a big bonfire on the beach, eat, drink, smoke dope, take off their clothes and dance, sometimes chant at the moon, if the moon was out. Howl like coyotes."

"And you were there?"

"I'll never forget it."

"Naked, bombed, chanting at the moon?"

"Well, yeah, so what?" I looked over at her. She was smiling.

"You never grew up," she said.

"I'll settle for it."

"And now you have to pretend to all those people, the lawyers, the judges, that you're just like they are."

87

"I try to fool as many people as I possibly can."

"It's too bad."

"Not really. The minute I can find someone willing to pay me a living wage to get drunk and stoned and dance naked on the beach, I'm outta here. Next time you're reading the classified ads, see what you can find."

*   *   *

The road was not out. The first three or four miles of it was even paved, which was something new. Then we passed a sign warning us that we were on a military reservation and subject to being stopped and searched. Suspicious activities, we were advised, could be met with deadly force.

Maria said "It's hard to imagine any normal person going past that sign just to spend a day at the beach."

"It's always been there, except for the part about deadly force."

"Which means what, exactly?"

"Well, my guess is they want to discourage terrorists.'

"By putting up a sign? I don't like it, deadly force. I think we should go back."

There was no safe place we could have turned around. We were descending a ridge in long switchbacks. The road had become a bumpy dirt two-track. Here and there washouts had been repaired with loads of broken concrete. Below was the Pacific Ocean, somewhere under a layer of mist.

Finally, we reached a broad cleared area on a bluff just over the beach. The mist was thickening. Through it could be seen the dim shapes of a dozen or so cars and campers, parked in no particular order. We had arrived. So had the fog, which was now the kind of Grade A industrial-strength fog you can get lost in. You couldn't even hear the surf, it was so dense. We sat in the cab of the camper and looked out at unvarying grey.

"This," Maria said, "is not my idea of Paradise."

88

It was hard to argue with her. It was late in the afternoon and further driving would be impossible until the fog lifted. Which it wasn't going to do, in my opinion. And as far as looking for the Lincoln Navigator, at that moment I couldn't have found the Lincoln Memorial, had someone cleverly transported it to Point Sal Beach State Park.

It wasn't so bad; we had groceries, ice in the cooler, a case of white Bordeaux, fresh water, propane for the stove. After a while we had some wine, turned on the radio to an oldies station and danced in the fog. More wine, then dinner, although later I didn't have a clear memory of what we ate. I did remember Maria taking out her .357 Magnum and loading it, leaving it on a little shelf over the stove. This sticks in my mind because when the sound of gunshots woke me, I looked first at the little shelf and saw that the gun was gone. Then I realized Maria wasn't there either.

18

If there were bodies out there in the kelp they were going to be hard to find. A persistent westerly had jammed a hundred feet or so of seaweed and floating junk into a tangle against the shore. The entire length of the beach as far as you could see in both directions, there it was, humping back and forth in the surge. Beyond that was the kelp. The water looked grey and bubbly, where you could see it. You could put anything out in that mess and it would vanish.

A dive boat was standing well off the beach. Skipper didn't want seaweed in his props. Two divers stood in the aft cockpit in full scuba gear, bright yellow wetsuits. They weren't buying it either. A helicopter hovered overhead, adding downdraft to the prevailing west wind. The sun was shining like nothing was wrong.

The beach was gravel. I had left my shoes in the camper and now regretted it. Maria and I stood just out of reach of the waves in a group of fifteen or twenty people, watching the show. Most of the spectators had the look of itinerant vehicle-dwellers; not bums but not workadaddies either. Some feathers and beads, but plenty of rumpled polyester. Distant echoes of the Big Bang that was Jack Kerouac's *On the Road*; highway wanderers attracted to Point Sal, the most isolated public beach in Central California. I overheard someone say that a rescue vehicle had skidded off the road coming in, and rolled.

Two Highway Patrol officers had arrived and blocked the road out with their car. They walked the beach in knee-length leather boots, questioning people. The young couple in the beads and feathers had decided the time was right for a walk up the beach, away from the stash they had buried in the sand when the cops appeared. They had been smoking reefers and sunbathing naked that morning. It's nice to know there are still some hippies around.

Later, Maria sat on a driftwood tree trunk embedded in the sand, looked out at the water. She was smoking a cigarette. We had hardly spoken to each other all day.

"Are we under arrest?" she said, in a tone that carried an echo of 'you're a lawyer - do something about it.' An accusatory echo. I found out early in my career that telling policemen you're a lawyer usually made things worse. I shrugged. We couldn't leave because the road was blocked by a Highway Patrol car, so were we 'arrested?' My concern was not about getting arrested; I figured that was coming. It was more the idea that Point Sal was such an isolated place, lacking even a sign telling visitors what was not allowed. So everything was allowed; things you liked and things you didn't like. It was the last frontier; nobody anywhere nearby except this ragged band of Point Salvadorans and two Highway Patrol officers. It would be a poor location to get into a beef with law enforcement, with people missing and presumed dead out in the water

91

somewhere, under acres of smelly floating seaweed. At that moment, my big hope was that Maria was not going to get sideways with the cops.

The helicopter had packed it in. A Coast Guard cutter was now out there near the dive boat. A Highway Patrolman walked toward us, and I put my hand on Maria's arm. Please don't bite him on the nose.

"You are Thomas McGuire?"

According to his name tag he was Patrolman Blakey. Tall, lean and deeply tanned over a moonscape of old acne scars. Aviator sunglasses. A little long in the tooth to still be a foot soldier. He had decided who the perpetrators were. I agreed with him that I was Thomas McGuire. How did he know?

"That Lincoln up there belongs to you?" He gestured up toward the bluff, where a black Lincoln Navigator squatted fatly amongst a litter of beat-up cars and campers, proudly overlooking Point Sal and the Pacific Ocean. Maria rolled her eyes.

"No."

"So how'd you get here, swim?" It was apparently a rhetorical question because he didn't wait for an answer. "Look, dickhead," he said in a sterner tone, then turned to Maria and said "Pardon me, ma'am." It was actually funny, he did it so smoothly. He turned back to me. "There are two men missing since last night. They came here a couple of days ago in your car. The one you say doesn't belong to you. You and the lady show up yesterday in a camper and argue with the people in the Lincoln. Sometime last night there are shots fired. There's blood on the ground by the Lincoln. There's blood on the beach. The two guys are gone. There's bullet holes in the Lincoln. Either of you want to tell me what happened?"

We looked at each other and shook our heads. So did Highway Patrolman Blakey as he reached for his handcuffs.

19

I tried to make a list of good things and bad things but found almost nothing to list under 'good,' except that the Lompoc PD holding cell was quiet and didn't stink. Bad news on this score was it was Friday night and drunks might yet show up screaming and puking and there would go the neighborhood. The Friday part was extra bad; there would be no Court until Monday morning, and since we were held on suspicion of murder we could not make bail off the bail schedule.

I had no idea what had happened down at the beach. I had gone outside after hearing shots fired, wandered around in the fog, saw nothing, heard nothing, hadn't wanted to call Maria's name, returned to the camper. She was there, in her bathrobe. As I watched she washed down two of my Xanax with a half-glass of white Bordeaux. I thought it was a poor time to point out that the label on the pills advised against mixing them with alcohol. I said something but she made a 'stop' gesture with her hand, and shook her head. She said 'tomorrow,' and crawled up into the minute cab-over sleeping area. I didn't see the .357 Magnum and wasn't about to go looking for it. For all I knew she had it under her pillow, loaded. I turned off the lights and locked the cab and the camper. I was glad I had brought enough pills to go around.

On the 'good' list was the call I had been allowed to make to Leland Brown's answering machine. For years I had been saying he would be the criminal lawyer I would call if I shot someone in broad daylight on Main Street. It had been part praise, since I thought Lee was the best in the city, and part joke. Right then I missed the joke.

My captors told me Maria was in 'the ladies side.' A delicate phrase under the circumstances. I wondered about the .357 Magnum, doubted that Maria would have thrown it away no matter what had happened. If she had fired it last night she had certainly cleaned it afterwards, though I hadn't seen her to do this. She had taken the whole collection of handguns out to the firing range the week before. Her hands would definitely test positive for gunpowder residue. I went on this way for a while, trying to sort 'good' things from 'bad' ones, until I found myself wondering whether Mr. Mahmoud would still be willing to take back the Lincoln and let me be, now that it had bullet holes in it. At that point I realized I was off the deep end.

The Deputy who came on duty late that night was kind enough to lend me his copy of *The Bridges of Madison County*. I read each page twice, slowly, to make it last. By Sunday morning I had decided it wasn't nearly as bad as some people said it was, although I thought this might be the result of some form of literary Stockholm Syndrome. That afternoon I was told I had a visitor, and Leland Brown appeared; confident, cheerful, unflappable, suit and tie. "Hi guy."

I said "They told me visiting hours weren't till Monday."

Lee smiled and rubbed two fingers together. "If Jackson

can't get it," he said, "Franklin sure will." I remembered Ray Charles singing this line. Then, it had been Lincoln and Jackson. Inflation.

I told him the entire story as he sat outside the bars of my cell. His face showed no reaction. Once in a while he would say "I see." It was his basic response to anything a client told him. You could have told Lee you dismembered your business partner and served him up as chipped beef on toast at a Boy Scout jamboree, and he would have said "I see."

When I had finished the entire saga of the Lincoln Navigator and what little I knew about the recent events at Point Sal Beach State Park, Lee called out "Rudy, you out there? And my jailor appeared with my personal possessions in one hand and the key to my cell in the other. Lee had walked me. On Sunday afternoon. In Lompoc. I said nothing until we reached his car. Then I said "How?"

He turned to me and gave a little smirk; Lee Brown the magician. If he explained it wouldn't be magic anymore.

I said "Lee, save it for the customers," forgetting that I was a customer too.

Turned out he was good friends with a local judge who liked to go fishing early Sunday morning. Lee had obtained a draft copy of my arrest report (a draft copy!) and met the judge at 5:00 a.m. as he walked down the dock to his sport fisher. It is a strange but irrefutable fact that people like to do favors for Leland Brown, to an extent that approaches the paranormal. And if you've got a judge who will do what you want, anything is possible. If a judge were ever to order pigs to fly we'd be picking them out of trees.

Lee started his car and said "It's all bullshit. Nobody saw you in contact with anyone in the Lincoln. Nobody saw you do anything. Everyone thinks somebody got killed, but all they have are some bloodstains on the sand. And somebody was shooting a gun. Big deal. They should come down to South Central LA on New Year's Eve. It's going to be a D.A. reject. You'd have walked on Monday so we figured why not today. I told the judge I'd bring you back if they wanted you."

"What about Maria?"

"That's not going to be so easy."

"Oh."

"I'll have to try to get bail set Monday morning, if I can. There's a witness statement that has her arguing with someone just outside the Lincoln. There's another witness statement I couldn't see, they say has more bad stuff in it. They say they can put a gun in her hand."

"They've got the Magnum?"

"Yeah. Why does she use a .357? I had a firearms guy on the stand once who told the jury you could break your arm from the recoil if you didn't know what you were doing."

"She shoots it all the time on the firing range. Hasn't broken anything yet."

"The cops want the DA to file a possession charge against her just for having it in the camper. They say it was recently fired, and she tested positive for gunpowder residue."

"I told you, she shoots handguns all the time."

"Well, they didn't know that. Do you know if she shot anybody?"

"No."

"She didn't tell you?"

"She sat on the beach all day staring at the water and smoking cigarettes."

"I didn't know she smoked."

"She doesn't." A pause. "Lee?"

"What?"

"If you were able to get me out, why'd you sit there for half an hour getting my story while I'm in a cell? I could have bought us lunch, for chrissakes."

"I wanted your complete attention. You want lunch now?"

"No."

We drove around until we found the camper in a police impound yard. Without Al Frankenstein standing next to it explaining what a gem it was, it looked like a clapped-out piece of junk, forlorn and dirty in the corner of a cyclone-fenced parking lot. Lompoc had lost its charm; today it sounded like a disease. Lompox.

Inside the camper, the ice in the cooler had melted and something stank. Lee waved and drove off in his plum-blue Jaguar. I found myself wishing I was him and not me. Too late for that.

It was the bacon that had gone bad. I threw it in a trash can under the watchful eye of a man in the booth at the gate. I fired up the machine and drove out onto the street. There was no way I was going to drive to Marina del Rey and back for court on Monday. I didn't have to dress up; I just had to be there for Maria

First, more groceries, ice for the cooler, and after a little thought, club soda, cube ice and brandy. Nothing fancy. A life on the open road. I drove back to Point Sal without thinking about it too much, musing about bodies in the kelp. As far as Lee Brown was concerned, there were no bodies, but I had stood on the beach and watched the show and I thought the kelp had looked right for it. Maria had looked right for it.

As I drove the final few hundred yards down the dirt track to the bluff over the beach I was thinking of Ariel's song from *The Tempest*:

> Full fathom five thy father lies;
> Of his bones are coral made;
> These are pearls that were his eyes:
> Nothing of him that doth fade
> But doth suffer a sea-change
> Into something rich and strange....

Gives me goose bumps every time.

*   *   *

That night there actually were people who built a bonfire on the beach, ate, drank, sang songs and got loaded. Woodsmoke and marijuana fumes floated up the bluff to where I sulked in the back door of the camper drinking brandy and soda. I was sure the bottle of brandy would have served as my ticket of admission to the festivities, but I wasn't in the goddamn mood, was I?

With the first faint morning light came the need to pee, and take a walk down the beach. As I walked I saw a group of three or four people far ahead, standing at the surf line, barely discernable in the half light. As I got closer the images clarified and I could see they were looking at a large dark lump floating in the surge. I figured it for a body. No surprise. Everyone knew there had to be a body, right? We pulled it out of the surf and laid it down on the sand. It was Amir Mahmoud; in a suit and tie. As we stood there, a tiny hermit crab crawled out of his nose.

20

As soon as I realized who we had pulled out of the water I withdrew all forces from Point Sal Beach State Park. Soon would come Patrolman Blakey who would wonder why I wasn't in jail and whether I could identify the deceased.

At the courthouse there was a sign on the door indicating that civil motions would be heard at eight-thirty, arraignments and prelims at ten. I parked across the street and waited in the camper. When I went back at nine forty-five they had been and gone. Lee had advanced the matter on the calendar and gotten Maria out somehow. The file was sealed by court order. Thirty minutes ago, and neither of them were around. They would have had to walk right past me.

I drove around Lompoc for awhile looking into coffee shops and diners. I couldn't stay. Give it enough time and someone would figure out who Amir Mahmoud was and why I might want him dead. It was a reflection on my abiding belief in my own bad luck at that point that it didn't occur to me that Mr. Mahmoud might have fallen in the water and drowned.

She was with Lee; where else could she have gone? I called Lee's office. His secretary said she'd call him on his cell but wouldn't give me the number. There hadn't been time for her to get to any place I could call. Fear and confusion turned into anger. I had called on Lee to help us, not to drive off with the only person in the world I cared about.

I got on US 1 headed south. It was the only way to LA. I had it up to eighty before I realized I was trying to overtake them without even knowing where they were. I could hear stuff clanking around in the camper when we hit a bump, which happened a lot. US 1 from Lompoc to Gaviota is an old road. I was pushing an old machine, trying to catch up with a this-years-model Jaguar XJ8 that I imagined was up ahead of me. What would I do if I saw them, run them off the road? Drive alongside, honking and waving? I had become the spurned husband in a bad country and western song; 'the city lawyer stole my sweetheart away.' This brought tears to my eyes.

I ran out of maudlin, adrenaline and gasoline about the same time. At a gas station in La Conchita I got a fillup and a chicken salad sandwich of dubious provenance, and a Pepsi. As I ate the sandwich I noticed that my hands were shaking.

The rest of the drive home was less exciting. I did not spot Lee's car. I thought of the seagull I had rescued; a big beautiful creature completely undone by a simple loop of twine. I remembered the morning they called me about the credit card and the Lincoln, and the fun I figured I was going to have sorting it out.

*   *   *

"How could you lose somebody in Lompoc?'
"When I got to the courthouse her case had already been

heard. She wasn't in custody and they were both gone."

"What'd he do for her?"

"I don't know. The file was sealed."

"Wazzat mean?"

"Means you don't get to look at it."

"Seven ball, corner."

I had drifted over to visit with Murray on my return to the Marina. The prevailing northwest wind was gusting strongly, raising a racket as hundreds of poorly secured halyards slapped and banged against hundreds of aluminum masts. *More Gefilte Fish* was bobbing and weaving on her end tie, but Murray's miraculous squirming pool table suited me fine, as did his company. Murray's seven ball did a slow 'S' roll and did not fall into the corner pocket.

He said "So where'd she go?"

"She rode down to LA with Lee."

"Maybe she couldn't find you."

"The camper was parked right outside the courthouse."

"With you inside?"

"Yeah. Six ball."

I attempted to overcome the rolling table with a show of force, but the six ball became airborne and landed on the cabin sole. Murray returned it, putting another even-numbered ball back on the table as a penalty.

"Ya shoulda kept an eye out."

"I was reading a goddamn book, Murray. I didn't think I was going to have to run out and catch her as she went by."

"Don't get excited. You think maybe this Arab of yours-"

"-He's not my Arab. Same with the car; people say 'this Lincoln of yours'."

"Just an expression, Tom."

"Yeah, well, before this started I had Maria, now she's gone and I've got a dead Arab and a Lincoln Navigator."

"With bullet holes in it, don't forget."

"That's a joke? You find this funny?"

Murray racked his cue. "C'mon outside," he said. "I

wanna smoke a cigar."

We went back to the aft cockpit and settled in a pair of upholstered wicker armchairs.

Murray said "You called her mother?"

"Twice."

"And the lawyer?"

"There was a message on the phone when I got on board. He had dropped her off at the boat, and didn't want to get between us by trying to explain things for her. He said 'She'll explain if she wants to.' Nice for him."

"The man's a lawyer, not a marriage counselor."

"Well, she was here. She's gone, the Harley's gone, some of her stuff, cosmetics."

"So give it a rest. You want my opinion?"

"Sure."

He poked his cigar upward toward the darkening sky. "You scare her."

I thought about that for a moment. "Did I ever tell you how we met?"

"Something about she was beating up some guy with a club?"

"She was bashing in the window of a new Oldsmobile with a piece of plumber's pipe."

"Oh yeah, now I remember. With some poor schlub inside the car probably pissing his pants."

"Oh, he had it coming, don't worry."

Murray laughed. "So you don't understand how you could scare someone like that?" He pulled his chair around so it was facing me. "Look, the two of you go off on her bike for a fun weekend down south and when you come back you're a drug mule, good for three to five guaranteed, assuming what was hidden in the car. Maybe ten, fifteen. They've got mandatory minimums now. Judges can't give you a break. Enough fun? No. Gotta have more fun? Get a camper and take her up to some beach in East Bumfuck where they shoot guns at night and pull stiffs outta the water, the stiff who's

103

investigating you." He sighed, noticed his cigar had gone out and relit it. "You're a magnet for trouble. You're like that old guy in the cartoons who can't see-"

"-Mr. Magoo."

"Right. Him. Lemme tell ya, Maria's not going on any more of your field trips 'till things settle down."

I gestured up the channel toward *Den Mother* on her end tie. "She used to live there."

"So go find her. You're a lawyer, talk her into coming back."

That seemed to be the plan.

I had a good look at Murray's latest aloha shirt, which depicted pieces of fried chicken on a black background. The chicken had posed a serious problem to the shirt's designer, appearing as a series of tan blobs only vaguely suggestive of food.

I said "I just remembered I've got cooking class tonight."

Murray looked surprised, but it was very simple; I didn't want to be alone.

21

It was a full house; lots of new faces. Victor Cannizzarro appeared in starched chef's whites, to light applause which he acknowledged with a bow. Considering the elaborate costume and the air of ceremony, I wondered if I was observing a cultural phenomenon in which cooking was gradually taking the place of organized religion. Instead of denominations like Protestant, Catholic, Jewish, the faiths would come to be identified by culinary regions; Northern Italian, Provencal, Szechwan, or by wines; *Les Amis de Gevrey-Chambertin*. The people in this room were excited because they knew they were going to learn something in a group experience, something that would leave them better off. Do many people feel this way in church? And if not, why not?

Cannizzarro cleared his throat, adjusted his new clip-on

microphone. "Friends," he said, "our little classes have become very popular." Applause. Another bow. "There are people here tonight from all walks of life..." He paused for effect. "...including law enforcement." Still not Julia Child, but he was improving. His reference to law enforcement caused a murmur and a good deal of glancing around. Which ones were the cops? And why had Vic let them in?

The wiseguys were out tonight, off to one side in their own section, all hairspray, grey silk and self confidence. Their response to Cannizzarro's announcement was to stifle grins and roll their eyes like a bunch of schoolboys who had put a snake in teacher's desk drawer.

Cannizzarro continued, "Tonight we gonna make *Arrosto di Vitello*, stuffed with prosciutto and sweet sausage." He had a large veal loin on the table in front of him, butterflied flat. "Now, this is good Italian food, make you strong." He gestured toward the back of the room. "You people inna government, you don't eat so good. You make a nice stuffed veal roast like this one, maybe you catch more bad guys."

Here and there in the crowd people were laughing, some looking around to locate the butt of Cannizzarro's jokes. It wasn't hard. Larry Hayden, Jerome the polite blond FBI agent and two other young suits sat in the last row, getting madder and madder. They weren't used to being taunted in public by the criminals they were supposed to catch and convict, and in front of a bunch of well-off civilians, too. They were looking at Larry for a signal and I could tell that in a moment they were going to get up and leave, to a combination of laughter and applause.

Which they did. The crowd loved it. 'Do you know what happened at my cooking class?' Cannizzarro stood behind his table, beaming, now more of a ringmaster than cooking instructor. If he had had a whip he would have cracked it.

"Hey fellas," he called to the retreating G-men, "give my regards to J. Edgar Hoover."

This got another good-sized laugh. I looked around for

106

the stooge, the one the Feds had left behind. After a few minutes I decided it was either the earnest emaciated young guy in a wheelchair or a businesslike black man in his forties with a gray brush cut, in an oversized camo field jacket. You had to hand it to somebody; if they were law enforcement it was a doozy of a setup. A politically correct reincarnation of Marshal Dillon and Chester.

The skinny guy in the wheelchair was wearing a blue-and-white plaid flannel shirt. He looked distinctly middle-American; the sincere blond crew cut, pouty immature expression. His lower body was covered with a tan blanket. He reminded me a little of the guy who blew up the Federal Building in Oklahoma City, except that guy squinted more and his eyes were closer together.

Now the black guy removed the loose camo jacket revealing a seriously overdeveloped upper body. Thigh-sized biceps, the generalized inflated lumpiness so prized by the steroid set. He wore a tee-shirt bearing the image of a snarling gorilla holding a barbell and the words 'World Gym.' The gray hair made a nice contrast with his dark skin. He had a mean look. Yet in spite of the muscles and the hairy eyeball he seemed vaguely bureaucratic.

Cannizzarro was looking at me. First he raised one hand a little, in welcome, than did an almost imperceptible combination of eye roll, chin and shrug. Not complaining, I thought. Why should he? His taunts and Larry's staged withdrawal had goosed the show; gotten it off the ground right at the beginning. For a hoodlum, Cannizzarro had plenty of stage smarts.

The stuffed loin of veal proceeded. Vic pureed sausage and combined it with egg, with breadcrumbs, with sage and parsley. If it had been music it would have been Beethoven. The wiseguys looked bored, but not the rest of the group; Brentwood ladies who lived on yogurt and organic vegetables evaluated Vic's veal loin with a prurient eye. Camo jacket and skinny took copious notes, as did many others. I imagined them back at the Federal Building attempting to figure out what secret messages had been concealed in the veal; what the breadcrumbs signified. Was there a mysterious underworld figure nicknamed 'The Veal?' I didn't think so.

Best odds were that Maria was in San Gabriel with her mother. The old lady had not thought much of me in the first place. Now, she was probably telling her daughter that events had proved her right; no good had come of our pairing. The finished *Arrosto di Vitello* went into the oven as its fully roasted twin appeared. Applause, then small samples of roast stuffed veal. I should have married her while I had the chance.

Up front, Vic had started with *Cacciucco Alla Livornese*, a kind of fish stew. I could see the heaps of clams, mussels, shrimp and lobster waiting their moment on stage. Maria and I would have spent the entire day, hunting, gathering, then preparing and eating such a dish. We would have made a weekend out of it. I contemplated a lifetime of lonely TV Dinners and almost broke down. I left the store and went out on the street to make a phone call. Maria, her mother said, was "no in casa."

*   *   *

On board *Den Mother* there were no messages waiting for me on the answering machine. I hadn't checked my e-mail for days, and there was a ton of spam waiting to be deleted. I clicked through offers of a cheaper mortgage, a bigger penis, better credit, until I found and opened one from Larry Hayden. The subject was "Thought You Might Be Interested In This" but when I opened it there was no text, just an indication of a file attachment, which I downloaded and opened. It was a picture of me at the wheel of a black Lincoln Navigator, with a date and some sort of identifying markings stamped across the bottom of the page. I was smiling and waving in the direction of the camera. I didn't have to check the date. I had only driven the damn thing once.

108

I looked at the image for a few moments then hit the 'reply' button on my e-mail screen and sent 'what does this mean?' After ten minutes I had no return e-mail, but the phone rang.

"Ever since 9/11, every vehicle through the checkpoint, we get an image of the driver. Don't noise it around."

"Larry, what does this mean?"

"It's part of homeland security."

"No, dammit, why'd you send me the picture? Who took it?" I had assumed that Lou Gizzi sent me after the Lincoln. Now it appeared the Government had been involved too. It made no sense to me.

Larry said "We need to talk. What was the name of that place we went to the last time?"

"Chinoise on Main?"

"Yeah. How about you take me there?"

"The last time I spent about a hundred forty dollars on a meal and a nice bottle of wine; brandy, even, and at the end you had me arrested, remember? Me and Maria both."

"Aw, that was years ago."

"So was the transfiguration of the Savior, but it's still widely remembered."

"I thought you were Jewish."

"On my mother's side. Don't change the subject. I'll go back to Chinoise with you on two conditions."

"You're in no shape to bar-"

"-You pay and I don't get arrested when it's over."

109

22

I drove the camper back to Frankenstein's Quality Cars, but I couldn't get the Eldo; it had been sold.

"And if you're thinking about the Volvo," Al said, "forget it. I've been leaving it in the sun with the doors open, but it still smells like a gym locker."

"I'm sorry."

"Fuck it. I'll sell it to somebody sooner or later."

"You could sell snow to Eskimos."

He was wearing a shimmering gray sharkskin suit and suspenders, which he snapped. "Everybody's got a talent. I sell cars."

What was I good at? "I need something a little beat-up, something I can drive to the East Side and not get noticed."

He flashed his Trotsky eyes at me. "You're gonna stake

111

somebody out? Never mind; try to keep this one dry."

*   *   *

I drove the Toyota to Pearl Street in San Gabriel, and parked. Al had done right by me; you would not notice this car if it ran you over. Early eighties, dented, dirty, downmarket repaint in an indeterminate color. Who could have unloaded this heap on Al? To further blend in I had acquired a Dodgers cap and a pair of mirror shades.

I was a block away from the Zaragoza family home and the plan was that Maria would have to walk by to do any local shopping, at which point I would emerge from the car and....that was as far as it went. I figured I'd think of something. I didn't figure that after half an hour *Señora* Zaragoza would come up behind me and start shouting and poking at the car with her cane, but that's what happened. Attacking cars seemed to run in the family.

If I continued to sit there she'd draw a crowd. If I got out of the car I'd probably get the cane-poke treatment. Lousy choices. I left.

I drove back, past the downtown freeway interchanges, and was traveling west on the Santa Monica Freeway when I thought I smelled something peculiar. I pulled the car into the breakdown lane and stopped, then pulled the lever under the dashboard that released the hood. As I stood next to the car it seemed as though fumes were escaping from under the hood, but when I opened it the entire engine compartment burst into flames. I got back a few feet and talked to a 911 operator on my cell phone, then I called Al Frankenstein.

"You remember that Toyota you loaned me?"

"What's that noise?"

"Traffic. You remember the Toyota?"

"What?"

"It's on fire."

"What?"

112

"It's burning."

"You set my car on fire?"

"Of course not."

"But you just said-"

"-I didn't set it on fire, it caught fire by itself. I was driving-"

"-Where are you?"

"Santa Monica Freeway."

"Where's the car?"

"Right in front of me."

"You're not hurt?"

"No, I'm fine. It's the Toyota that's having a bad day. Oh look, here comes the fire engine."

"It's totaled, right?"

"The whole thing is burning."

"Great."

"You're happy?"

"I gave some schmuck two hundred dollars for it on a trade-in. Now I can sell it to the insurance carrier for wholesale Blue Book. On fire it's worth a grand to me. You got the kinda cell phone with a camera?"

I had the wrong kind of cell phone. I stood there for a while watching the firemen put out the burning Toyota, late afternoon rush hour traffic surging ferociously by in the next lane. Then my phone rang, and I thought maybe this was going to be the last day I'd carry one around.

It was Leland Brown, calling to tell me he couldn't represent me any more.

"You'll never guess where you've reached me, Lee."

"Where are you?"

"I'm standing in a breakdown lane on the westbound Santa Monica Freeway watching my car burn."

"Oh. I see."

"Well, I doubt you're getting the full flavor of it."

"Listen, they've got a body but they don't know who it is yet. The only slugs they have came out of the Lincoln, and

113

they're useless, too deformed to match to a firearm. You say there was dense fog that night?"

"Absolutely."

"So does Maria. They've got a witness who can see through fog, I guess. He's got Maria arguing with the victim just before shots were fired. And she tested positive for gunpowder residue. So they figure she had motive, means and opportunity, plus she had discharged a gun recently, and that's what they're going to go with."

"How about me?"

"Conspiracy, maybe. I don't know. There's a couple of witnesses I haven't talked to. Maybe they figure they can get you to testify against her. I'm just calling to tell you there's no way I can represent both of you. When you get a lawyer we can do a joint defense agreement, if it gets that far, but for the time being if you get a tap on the shoulder, you're on your own."

"But I'm the one who brought you into this."

"You're not the one getting indicted."

It sounds really stupid but I felt excluded, as if Lee had just stolen my girlfriend. In a way, he had.

23

Larry Hayden sat at a little table for two against the south wall at Chinoise on Main. It was early; the noise level in the room was still bearable. As I approached he saw me, moistened his lips, rehearsing what he was going to say. Even when he'd been my colleague, driving a desk at the US Attorney's office, he'd been like this, frowning at his yellow pads; writing out our strategies in elaborate detail. He wouldn't have survived six months in private practice.

He was thinner than I remembered. The familiar standard-issue grey wool suit hung loosely. The material of his tie was worn through at the top of the knot, just below his chin where stubble had abraded it. He looked worn, but not older; one of those people who age cannot wither because they have never bloomed.

I took a seat at the table. I said "Looking for the bread and butter?"

"I asked. They don't put any out."

Something to do with your hands until you could get a drink. I remembered he used to chew on pencils. 'Bring this man an Eberhardt Faber Number Three.'

He read the menu, his face expressing the mixture of contempt and envy that the spectacle of my imagined lush life style always seemed to evoke.

"Foie Gras," he said. "What's that?"

"Goose liver."

"Isn't that where they stick a tube-"

"-Behave yourself."

We both got vodka, which eased things a bit.

I said "Start with the picture." He looked startled; I had interrupted his train of thought. "The picture of someone who looks like me, driving an SUV, a Lincoln."

"Right." He assumed a look of mild indignation. "It was full of drugs. You drove it across the border into the United States. It's a major felony."

"How do you know all this?"

"Well, it's kind of hard to explain." He looked around helplessly, as if there was someone nearby who might help him explain. He then excused himself and went to the men's room. I ordered us both another drink. Larry was paying.

When he returned he poured the remains of his first drink into the second without hesitating. "You see," he began after a silent moment with the vodka, "my people have a certain interest here..." He contemplated the nearly naked back of a young lady seated facing away from us. "A certain interest."

"And you're going to tell me what it is?"

He looked startled. "What it is?"

"The interest you have."

"Not exactly."

"Then let's order. Are you going to let me order a bottle of Sancerre, like last time?"

117

"Of course."

"And not arrest me when we're done?"

He thought for a moment. "I don't see why. Should I?"

We ate crispy fried oysters on the half shell, dressed with salmon eggs, a house specialty.

"Tell me, Larry," I said, "was it heroin or cocaine?"

He had been licking the juice out of the bottom of an oyster shell, which he put back on his plate.

"Heroin or cocaine?"

"In the SUV you say I was driving in the picture."

"Oh, it was you all right. If not, why would you be here?" The smug old prosecutor. "I'd just as soon you didn't know what was in the vehicle. It makes your story less plausible."

"Unless you tell it."

"Well, yes. We can supply all the details, if it becomes necessary."

"Larry, this is the worst bunch of crap. Just tell me what you want."

For the first time that night he looked focused. "Cooperation,' he said. "Yours and your girlfriend's." He poured himself a generous portion of the Sancerre. "The Department has invested a great deal of time and money in the Santa Barbara area."

We ordered stir-fried lamb in radicchio leaves, then a whole deep-fried catfish with ginger. Another house specialty. The restaurant had filled up. The noise was overwhelming. We were leaning toward each other over the tiny table, whispering like two conspirators. I noticed the end of his tie was in his dinner plate, soaking up the ponzu sauce that came with the catfish.

I thought of Amir Mahmoud lying dead in his soggy suit on the sand at Point Sal Beach. I said "You don't want our lawyers poking around up there?"

"Right. Or you, either. There's too much at stake to risk it over a stupid credit card dispute."

"You don't want anyone to know just exactly what

happened that night?"

"Plenty of people know."

"Care to give me their names and phone numbers?"

He did not offer a reply. He had managed to flag down a waiter and order an elaborate dessert, which had arrived and now engaged his complete attention.

I sipped the remains of my wine and waited for his response. When nothing was forthcoming I said "Leland Brown tells me Maria will be indicted by the Santa Barbara County Grand Jury."

"I'm sorry to hear that."

"Yeah. He says I may be next."

Larry was busily spooning up *creme brulee*. "If you cooperate," he said, "we'll probably be able to do something for you."

"Right now Maria's the one who could use some help."

He made a face that was probably a sneer twenty years ago when he still had some moxie. The anxious ambition that had once driven him now seemed like a trick learned long ago by an old dog.

"We'll play it out," he said, "and see how it goes."

It sounded like something he had practiced in front of a mirror; maybe a line from a favorite movie. I didn't know the next line, so I made one up.

"I know you'll take care of us."

He seemed happy to hear this. He went on eating his dessert. Larry had become a very literal-minded person, if he had ever been anything else, and he had just flunked my bullshit test. 'Take care of us' indeed. Against all reason, he believed I trusted him. I thought it might give us certain advantages, depending on what happened next.

24

When I got back to the Marina I saw the Harley in the parking lot. Down at the boat there was a post-it on the dockside salon hatch, on which Maria had written 'I'm at the Jolly', which meant The Jolly Lobster, the seafood joint fifty feet down the seawall from our gangway.

She was at the bar, wearing her go-to-work blue suit and a far-off look.

I stood behind her and said "Lose your key?"

She turned around. Her eyes were red. I felt stupid for my remark. I said "Buy you a drink, fair lady?" which got the merest glimmer of a smile.

She was drinking Scotch, which I found alarming. She never drank distilled spirits, but it was encouraging, too. Possibly, she intended to stay the night. Maria claimed Scotch and motorcycles didn't mix. I knew a lot of people who would have disagreed with her. Former clients, mostly.

She said "Lee told me not to talk with you, but I want you to know what happened."

I took a seat next to her at the bar and ordered Pelligrino water. I said "Whatever it was, it doesn't have to mean-"

"-I went out in the dark to take a pee, that's all."

"With the .357 Magnum?"

A sigh. "You drove me there, remember? You said it was the wildest place in the West, or whatever you said. Drunken orgies. It was dark. It was so foggy I could hardly see my hand in front of my face. I had no idea who might be out there, and I was naked except for my bathrobe."

"So what happened?"

"I went off to the side where there were no cars parked and squatted down. I was almost finished when someone put a bright light on me and said 'throw down your weapon and lie on your stomach."

"You had the gun in your hand?"

"It wouldn't go in the pocket of the robe."

"So what'd you do?"

"I shot out the light."

"Did it occur to you to do what was asked; throw down the gun and lie on your stomach?"

"First of all, I was peeing. Once you start, it's a commitment."

"I get it."

"Second, who sneaks up on ladies who are relieving themselves in the dark and embarrasses them with a spotlight? If I wanted attention I'd do it on stage."

"In LA you could get work."

"So I shot out the light."

"Hit anything besides the light?"

"It's hard to say. I might have."

"What happened after that?"

"Two or three more gunshots. Some men yelling. The fog was too heavy to see anything. I went back to the camper. I figured they couldn't see me and I couldn't see them, so I'd get in the camper and they wouldn't know where I was."

"They?"

"Oh, yes. For sure. There were at least two voices, maybe three."

"But you have no idea who it was who told you to throw the gun down and lie on your stomach."

"No, but he was probably a bachelor or he wouldn't have made such ridiculous demands."

"Well, you showed him."

"Don't make fun of me. I've thought about it a lot, tried to reconstruct the moment I shot at him, at whoever. It was the sound of his voice; if I hadn't shot first he would have killed me."

"And the chances of your convincing anyone of that-"

"-are zero. I know. But I'm alive."

She looked like she was about to cry, but didn't. After a moment she finished her Scotch, ordered another, then reached into her purse for a pack of cigarettes that wasn't there. She wouldn't have been allowed to smoke in the restaurant anyway. The new purity.

I said "Are you staying on the East Side?"

"My mother is furious with you."

"I figured. And Lee is telling you to stay away from me."

She drank off half of her second drink. "Tom, he's telling me I'm accused of murder."

"Maybe we'll get adjoining cells."

"It's not funny. No, I'm going to do this by the numbers. And my mother would never want to see me come back here, regardless."

"Your mother never liked me."

"Well, now she's got a good reason, doesn't she? I know I don't have to do what she tells me to, but this time I don't feel like breaking with her. We've been a lot closer since Pop died and I don't want to spoil it. I feel safer there."

"How old is she now?"

"Eighty-seven, but don't let on that you know. And don't

assume she's weak. She gets things done. She saw the *curandera* about us and I'm pretty sure they put a spell on you.

"They put a spell on me? Like Screamin' Jay Hawkins?"

She put a few bills on the bar for the drinks, and made a 'let's go' gesture. Outside on the seawall she said "Many people in my community believe in these things. You say it's superstition, but that's just a word."

"It works?"

"She had a spell put on the boys who shot my brother."

"What happened?"

"They were arrested and convicted. They're all still in prison."

"And that proves exactly what?"

"Don't get excited. They're folk customs, not laboratory experiments. If they work, I think it's because people believe in them. Without people to believe, the spirits die."

"They teach you that at UCLA?"

"Be nice, Tom. I'm the only daughter. She just wants to protect me."

"So I'm under a spell?"

"I wouldn't worry about it. The *curandera* is there to help; to recapture a husband's lost love for his wife, to help you recover from an illness. In your case I think she was looking for something to separate us, to keep us apart."

I thought about the burning Toyota. "Lemme tell you about something that happened to me yesterday afternoon..."

*   *   *

Maria was not impressed with the story of the burning car. She considered that I deserved it for refusing to buy a real car and, instead, drawing from the never-ending supply of Al Frankenstein's second-hand rolling stock.

"Lee has a lovely Jaguar," she said. "Maybe you should get one. Don't blame my mother because some crummy Toyota caught on fire."

Maybe I should drive a Jaguar. My clients would like that, but I liked the idea of disposable cars. Like Kleenex; you use it, you throw it away. Why make payments on Kleenex?"

Then she asked me what happened to the camper and why I was driving the Toyota in the first place, so I had to tell her about my excursion to San Gabriel, *Señora* Zaragoza's cane-poke assault, and my retreat under fire.

She said "You weren't going to tell me about it?"

"Maybe later. How did she know I was there?"

She laughed. "My mother knows everyone in the area. She knows the names of their dogs and cats. She knows the cars they drive." Then her expression changed. "Don't come out to San Gabriel, Tom. Not until this whole thing is resolved. I didn't realize she'd seen you and your car. It's not a good idea for you to create any more occasions."

"Occasions for what?"

She didn't respond. We walked to where the Harley was parked. I kissed her. She mounted the machine, fired it up and was gone, two scotches and all.

The next morning I broke a shoelace getting dressed, cut myself shaving, then went into court and lost a slam-dunk Motion I had filed. I thought of *Señora* Zaragoza and the *curandera.*

25

I made a cup of coffee and took it up to the bridge, where I sat at the control panel and tried to make some sense of recent events. Some of the pieces didn't fit. Some of them were missing. Larry said the body we found in the surf that morning had been shot. By whom? Assuming someone didn't carry the deceased Mr. Mahmoud to the place we found him in the surf, what had he been doing at Point Sal State Beach? Best guess, he was doing what we were doing; looking for the Lincoln Navigator. A real hands-on guy, he wanted to glom onto it and drive it home triumphantly, like Caesar entering the gates of Rome with the spoils of war. Maybe it would get him a pay raise. I could go with that. And had he brought the handgun I had noticed in the front seat of his car? A good chance of that, too. He brought it to the car wash, didn't he? And on the beach he encountered people who didn't appreciate the attention. That was a sure thing. Who were they? I had the impression from things that Ted and Debbie had told me that Point Sal State Beach was notorious; possibly a smuggler's drop-off point. I remembered Larry Hayden telling me that there were plenty of people who knew exactly what happened that night. I could really use that information.

*　　*　　*

I met Maria after work in Chinatown, a block from her office at Adult Protective Services. This time it was her idea. It was a long way from the Marina but I figured she wasn't going to come out to see me. Under the circumstances I wasn't going to attempt another car trip to San Gabriel, being under a spell and potentially subject to *Señora* Zaragoza's cane-poke treatment. I didn't think Al Frankenstein would understand if I burned down another one of his cars. I didn't know why Maria had asked me to meet, and I was afraid it was so she could tell me goodbye forever. But I had to go.

Yang Chow was the kind of Chinese restaurant with fantastic food, a tiny sign out front, and blacked-out windows. If you didn't know it was there, that was fine with them.

She was at the bar when I arrived, drinking something clear with bubbles in it. She looked up as I approached, with an expression on her face that I couldn't read. Then I could; she looked wary. I ordered Scotch.

She said "I told my mother I'm working late."

"Did she believe you?"

"No."

"Please come back."

"No."

"I'm living on take-out. I'm gonna die."

A small smile that faded. "You won't die right away."

I said "You know who told me to stay away from Santa Barbara? My old buddy Larry Hayden. We had dinner at

128

Chinoise. He paid."

Maria said "He paid? That's alarming."

A pause. The bartender brought me a stingy little Scotch rocks.

She said "You ate at Chinoise. I thought you said you were living on take-out."

"I miss your cooking."

"How romantic."

I took a little sip of my Scotch and it was gone. I said "You're being set up."

"That's what Lee Brown says. He wanted me to talk to you about it. He says the witness statements sound wrong. They've got people seeing me do all sorts of things I didn't do, and nobody could have seen me anyway."

"Because of the fog."

"Right. But that works both ways. I've been thinking about this ever since it happened."

"What do you mean?"

"I must have shot that guy. It's the only logical explanation."

The room seemed to lurch. I understood now why she had looked so apprehensive.

"You've been thinking about it," I said, "and that's what you figured out?"

"Maybe so."

"It's what your mother and her witches told you to tell me, isn't it? Maybe I won't want you now?"

"Oh Jesus! I'm sorry I ever told you about the *curandera*. Nobody's telling me what to say."

"You're sorry. I'm sorry. Let's have a sorry contest. Did you tell this story to your lawyer?"

"Not yet."

"Are you going to?"

"I haven't made up my mind. I might."

"Well, watch your step. Lee's got too much class to tell you to lie on the stand. Oh, by the way, I've got a Grand Jury

129

subpoena coming from Santa Barbara. Now I'll have to testify. Technically, if they ask me, I'll have to tell them about this conversation."

"Good thing you don't have too much class to lie on the stand."

I hate it when they think faster than I do. The harpoon went right in the front and out the back; it would take days to pull it out. I tried to look at her face but she was focused down toward her drink with a studious 'nobody home' look.

I said "Ok, I understand. I should stop trying to manage things."

I turned my attention to the bartender and attempted to explain to him that if he combined two stingy little Scotches in one glass he'd have a double, which was what I wanted. He said he understood, and brought me two stingy little Scotches. I felt everything important in my life was slipping away from me.

*   *   *

Den Mother was like a tomb without her, an urban shipwreck. She wouldn't take my calls at work and her mother wouldn't put her on the phone at home. When I considered sending her an e-mail I realized I knew her screen name and password, and could log on to her account. Under the circumstances, what choice did I have? The alibi of every spineless shit in history, but there it was. I'm not going to lie to you.

She had cleaned out her inbox, so all the e-mail was Old Mail or Sent Mail. It was also mostly in Spanish. I hadn't expected that. I have just enough Spanish to order in a restaurant, so the e-mail didn't occupy me for long. I did notice quite a few communications to and from addresses using an ISP called ojinaga.com, which sounded like it would be in Mexico. I saw one Sent Mail with a file attachment, which I opened. It was a picture of me at the controls of Den Mother. I remembered the trip to Catalina when Maria had taken the picture. Who had she sent it to? An address on the ojinaga server. A girlfriend?

I was not about to create tangible evidence of my sins by printing out Maria's e-mail, but I did locate and note all the TIFs, the temporary internet files that identified the websites she had visited. This, I rationalized, was not so personal an invasion as reading her e-mail.

The websites linked to other websites she had visited, and I spent a couple of hours surfing the Net. Many of the websites were in Spanish, but some were not. One of the first things I learned was that Ojinaga was a town in the province of Chihuahua, and that it was a center of *brujeria* and *curanderismo*, terms which can be loosely translated as 'witchcraft,' although the word does not convey the full flavor. I learned that in Mexico, at least, there is little that is quaint or old fashioned about these beliefs. I read about a well-known *curandero* (basically a 'good witch') who was killed when he was brought to Tijuana to remove a hex from a person who had been cursed by a *brujo* (a 'bad witch') in the hire of powerful *narcotraficantes*. When they discovered the *curandero* had removed a curse from one of their enemies after they had paid a lot of money to have it put on, they killed him. This was not the culture that produced *The Wizard of Oz*, or the song *Ding Dong the Witch is Dead*.

Despite the odd business with the burning Toyota I had little fear than a Mexican witch was going to do something to harm me. I was less certain about Mrs. Zaragoza. Practicing law had taught me there is no such thing as a harmless elderly lady.

131

26

A short conversation with Al Frankenstein convinced me I didn't need a Jaguar like Lee's. He told me I could buy a new one for sixty grand or so, right off the showroom floor. A nice big fat one, like Lee's. I nixed that idea. Al kindly offered to buy me a used one at the wholesale auction, any year, mileage and condition. I wasn't sure. A childhood in the Bronx had bypassed the car culture for me entirely, and now, as an adult, cars just didn't make my dingus tingle. Without that, you're wasting your money. Now, if you want to tell me you're going to install a twelve-volt icemaker on board *Den Mother* I'll listen, though I don't actually need one. Boat jewels.

I wandered among Frankenstein's Quality Cars and tried to think. Larry was trying to tell me something about Santa Barbara, but didn't want to get too specific. Maria had acted strangely in the fog at Point Sal, but couldn't tell me what had happened there. Or wouldn't tell me. Meanwhile my attention span was shot and I was sleeping badly, and sleeping alone. And forget the Thai takeout; don't even mention it, or the spell I was supposed to be under. Mexican magic. It was amazing how unglued everything had become, and how tricky. And who said there wasn't more of it to come?

I needed to do something decisive, so I made a phone call, packed a bag, and cabbed it to Santa Monica. There, I took a Greyhound to Santa Barbara, where Ted and Debbie were waiting to take me for a boat ride.

I had my go-to-sea kit, which consisted of a hand-held VHF marine radio, oranges, whiskey, chocolate, beef jerky, foul weather gear, watch cap and a heavy sweater. I also had an expensive-looking pair of night vision binoculars I had bartered for an old Kelvin-White compass at a marine swap meet.

From the bus station in Santa Barbara I took the tram down State Street and across the waterfront to the Marina. I walked out on the seawall to the commercial dock, where I could see Ted on board his trawler *Katie*. He was a large man with a red beard. Like many commercial fisherman I have met he was serious-minded, short spoken and short tempered. I liked him for it. It is easier to spend time with people who don't talk a lot. And as for the short temper, it was a quality I thought I could use; I had been passive for too long, a habit I picked up in childhood, and I was getting a little impatient with it. Maybe I needed a role model.

Ted was ripping the planks off *Katie's* deck, and replacing them, working fore to aft. There was a neat stack of boards in the bow, and a pile of splintered old ones on the dock. *Katie* was a heavy forty-six foot trawler, purpose built, with a high wheelhouse, high freeboard forward, low aft, and a long open aft deck for the trawl net, the drum it wound up on, and the assortment of gear necessary to extract shrimp from the sea. Ted's father had built the boat fifty years ago. When the hull started to deteriorate, Ted and his father had encased its timbers in ferrocement. Now, when things needed to be done, Ted did them himself. Give him a bale of steel wool and he'd knit you a stove.

The deck would be finished by morning. We could go out then. Ted turned down my offer to help with a bemused look and pointed me towards a bunk below, where I settled in with the new Donald Westlake that had kept me company on the way up.

I called my office from my cell phone and learned I had no calls. I was informed I had a registered letter from the Santa Barbara District Attorney, and declined the offer to have it opened and read to me. For the time being I'd worry about it in the abstract.

I napped. When I awoke it was dark and Ted was gone. The deck looked finished. I wandered up to the seawall and watched the tourists, then bought fried clams and beer, which I took down to *Katie's* tiny galley. The sky looked good for tomorrow. I could have turned on my handheld and gotten the NOAA marine weather forecast, but they use a computer-generated voice that gives me the creeps and, anyway, it wasn't my boat.

The diesel woke me. Ted was at the helm, docklines away, easing us out of the slip. Debbie was below, stowing supplies in the galley. At the gas dock I paid for a fillup of diesel. Neither of them had asked why I wanted to take a boat ride to Point Sal and spend the night there. They were shrimpers. I was a lawyer. I had done them favors and now they were doing me one. I was hoping it didn't have to get more complicated than that. It was a dumb thing to hope.

Debbie offered me coffee. I accepted. Outside the breakwater we bounced off some short steep rollers which smoothed out as we got into deeper water. It was fair and sunny. The diesel roared and stank. I thought I could spend the rest of my life this way.

Ted had the helm, then Debbie, then I drove the boat for a while. The weather was coming from the north. The autopilot

135

did most of the work, constantly correcting our course to windward. All I needed to do at the wheel was to make sure we didn't bump into anything and keep an eye on several temperature and pressure gauges. When we got to a waypoint on the GPS Ted punched in a new one. We passed Point Conception by noon, keeping a steady eight knots. Point Arguello by five or so. I slept a lot. So did we all.

When we arrived at Point Sal we had been under way for twelve hours and everyone was tired. It was full dark, which made finding the anchorage difficult. Ted backed and filled and said nothing, peering into the radar screen and depth indicator until he was satisfied we were in the right place, then dropped the anchor, backed down on the anchor rode, and killed the engine. We were alone in the anchorage. After a day's worth of diesel roar the silence was unbelievable.

A heavy dew was falling, and we all went below to avoid being soaked. In the galley a single 12-volt lamp cast deep shadows on us as we sat around a small built-in table.

Ted said "I didn't ask you before, but are you expecting anything to happen here?" He wasn't quite scowling, but he was used to being Captain, and I think he generally didn't like doing things other people told him to do, particularly without an explanation.

I said "Are you?"

"Well," he said, "it's like this. If I'm fishing around here and maybe I want to drop the hook for an hour or two, or for the night, if I see anyone here I don't know I just go on by."

"Why?"

"Because I like to mind my own business, that's why. How about you. You've got business here?"

I told him that I didn't know. "A while ago there was an incident here, at the beach."

He said "We heard. Somebody drowned."

"I don't know. Maybe not." They stared at me. "Maria and I were down here in a camper the night before it happened. There were shots fired."

They looked at each other. *Katie* represented their livelihood. Had I put them in harm's way? It hadn't occurred to me, but now it did. By not telling them the story I had effectively lied to them.

Ted said "Are you in trouble?"

"I don't know yet. But Maria is. They think she killed someone."

Debbie said "Jesus." She looked out a porthole into the darkness. I could feel Ted getting angry.

"Anybody does any shooting," he said, "they better count on getting back more than they give." He gestured to a semi-automatic rifle in a bracket on the bulkhead. A 30.06, maybe, but I'm an unreliable judge.

I got out my kit and almost offered them whiskey before I remembered that neither of them drank, so I took the whole thing topsides and sat in the wet. Give them a chance to tell each other what an asshole I was.

To the naked eye there was some amount of activity on the beach; a campfire and shadows when someone would walk in front of it. The night vision binoculars were useless. They transformed the campfire into a blinding flare of light, and turned the darkness into an interesting abstract pattern of bright greens and yellows. No amount of tweaking would improve their performance, nor the application of more scotch to the operator.

The cliff behind the beach caught the sound of the light surf, and echoed it back as a low sustained hiss. The air was thick with dew. When the wind was just right you could hear faint music. *Katie* rose and fell gently at anchor. To the west I noticed the running lights of another vessel, and I went below to tell Ted.

In the galley I could see by their faces I had been elected Most Unpopular on this cruise. Ted had taken the rifle from its bracket and now held it in his lap. When I told them someone seemed to be approaching our anchorage he launched himself up the companionway, rifle in hand, and I braced myself for the

137

tirade that some hapless recreational boater was about to experience. This did not turn out to be what happened.

The approaching vessel was now about a hundred feet away to seaward. It put a bright light on us and someone using a loudhailer said "Ahoy the trawler."

Ted motioned me into a shadow of the deckhouse.

More from the loudhailer; "Ahoy the trawler. This is HTS vessel Montana. Your vessel is within the Pacific Missile Range. You are in danger."

Ted cupped his hands and shouted "Bobby, is that you?"

Silence.

To me, Ted said "It's Bobby Cabral. He's a liar and a thief. He won't bother us. Watch." Then he shouted "Bobby, this is Ted DeSantis on *Katie*. Nobody's shooting off any missiles tonight, so get your ass out of here and turn out the light or I'll shoot it out."

The light went out.

Ted said "Sumbitch works for HTS. He's a range monitor for the Air Force. When they're gonna launch a missile at Vandenberg they've got a contract with his boss to put a bunch of boats out here to warn people off, get them out of the area. But what he does mostly is pull other fishermen's pots and steal what's inside.

"Lobsters?"

"Sometimes. Mostly crabs or spot prawns. If he finds boats around the buoys he wants to pull, he gives them this happy horseshit about being in the missile range and how they gotta leave."

"Are there pots around here?"

"Plenty."

Bobby Cabral was gone, the lights of his trawler faint dots in the mist to westward. Over the ridge above Point Sal Beach I could see the headlights of a car negotiating the switchbacks down the hill toward us.

Debbie came up from below and stood next to Ted, with the rifle between them. I realized that commercial fishermen work in completely isolated conditions, and that a cargo of the right seafood can be worth thousands. It didn't take much to put these people on a war footing.

I said "Who would buy seafood from a thief?"

Ted snorted. "Other thieves. There's one distributor he uses. No one else will touch him. And if you catch him pulling your pots, people say better leave him alone."

Debbie said "When Pop was fishing, if he saw you around his buoys he'd shoot at you. Not to kill you, just to make a point."

Ted said "That's not the way I do it. If I see one of my pots on someone else's deck he's going to the hospital. And I wouldn't care if it was Bobby. Someone's gonna stomp that man sooner or later. That boat that was just here? You couldn't see it in the dark but he runs a Bertram 46, only one I've ever seen with a refrigerated fish hold and an electric deck winch for pulling pots. That boat was made to be a rich man's toy. You couldn't touch it for three hundred grand."

I said "He paid for that with seafood?"

Debbie said "No. I heard on the dock his distributor loaned him the money. Wheelchair Jack."

I said 'Skinny kid?"

Ted gave me a surprised look. "You know him?"

"I saw him in my cooking class."

*   *   *

There were things I should have told them in advance and didn't, and now Ted and Debbie were not talking to me. I had thought maybe I would go ashore after dark, but Ted was not going to make his inflatable available. It was secured to the wheelhouse hardtop. I didn't bother asking. He wouldn't say no but there would be some problem, and we both would know why.

Debbie heated up a canned beef stew and offered me some, but I declined. Canned beef stew is not suitable for people living in close quarters. You can do perfectly well at sea with an orange, some beef jerky, whiskey, and a chocolate bar. All the basic food groups.

I sat aft on a hatch cover, pretending I wasn't there. After a while the moon came out and I could see the beach; no activity, the same kind of beat-up cars and campers parked on the bluff as the last time. Fire allowed to burn itself out around midnight. No singing, no dancing, no wild orgies that I noticed. I watched the beach until two in the morning before anything interesting happened, then a dark shape appeared to seaward, moving slowly toward the beach. From its size it could have been an inflatable, but it was hard to tell. It might have been drifting except there was an offshore breeze. Binoculars didn't help much. When it reached the beach the secret of its travel against the wind was revealed to be a scuba diver, who emerged from the surf next to whatever he had been towing in. It looked like a raft. Two people walked down to the surf line to meet the diver and spent a few minutes there. My night vision binoculars clearly identified the people as three greenish-yellow blobs. I couldn't make out what they were doing. Then the diver reentered the water and the raft began its slow journey across the kelp and offshore into the darkness. Was Bobby Cabral out there somewhere?

I waited, and in about a half-hour the raft reappeared, inbound again. This time I was ready, with a mask, fins and snorkel I had located in an equipment locker in the wheelhouse. I would have asked permission but the Captain and First Mate were forward in the tiny forepeak cabin, presumably asleep. I had forgotten to bring a bathing suit, and had to make do with my jockey shorts.

When the raft was about halfway between *Katie* and the beach I eased myself off the transom into the water. It was much colder than I had imagined it would be. Something else I hadn't anticipated was the need to negotiate the kelp, which was dense and tangled. It took a modified slither to accomplish this, and induced some moments of intense claustrophobia.

The fins, in particular, liked to hang up on the kelp and had to be pulled free every few feet. Swimming in the ocean at night can be frightening. It must be genetic. Swimming in a freezing cold ocean at night amid clinging underwater obstructions caused an emergency all-hands alert to go off in my head. This nighttime kelp-swimming was the kind of thing that Maria would come along on my excursions to try to prevent.

I was able to get within fifty feet or so of the next surfline encounter; close enough to identify the raft as a black Zodiac inflatable, and the cargo was a series of waterproof rubber bags. The diver was wearing a full wetsuit, including a black neoprene hood. There was no way to tell who he was. The faces of the two men on the beach were also impossible to see in the shadows, but there's no mistaking a large camo field jacket, and, if you're looking for it, the exaggerated muscular development of a dedicated bodybuilder.

*　　*　　*

We left at first light. Ted looked grim, said little. The ride back was not going to be fun. A small boat at sea is a wretched place to have a serious falling out with your companions. After a while I think Debbie felt bad about it.

"It's not your fault," she said. We were below, Ted up in the wheelhouse. "He doesn't like to go there."

"Point Sal Beach?"

"He says it's a difficult anchorage, but there's more to it than that."

"Bobby Cabral?"

"Yes."

"Wheelchair Jack?"

She looked up toward the wheelhouse. "If you get in that guy's face he'll have somebody sink your boat. It's happened."

"It's not just about crab pots, is it?"

"No. Sometimes when we're out at night, we've seen boats pulling pots that don't belong to them. Bobby's pots.

141

Once we found a package in one of our pots. Ted didn't even open it. He threw it overboard. We thought it was probably drugs and somebody put it there by mistake."

I said "they're using the crab pots to bring in drugs?"

She looked away. "That's all I'm going to say about it. Ted would kill me."

27

"If you're gonna talk to me about people turnin' into birds, forget it. Talk about somethin' else."

"I didn't say it actually happened, it's just that in this belief system -"

"-Except my sister married a guy from Brooklyn who basically turned into an ape after she married him. A tout at the track. A hot walker. Stunk like a pig, drunk all the time. She hadda divorce the putz."

"Having an ape for a brother-in-law doesn't count."

"Whatever." Murray shrugged. "You're the expert."

I had invited him to dinner on board because I had never mastered the art of eating dinner alone. I knew a few food tricks from watching Maria; split a papaya in half and fill the halves with bay shrimp in a tarragon mustard vinaigrette. Bread

143

catfish filets with a mixture of Zatarain's spicy seafood breading and Panko and sauté them lightly in a mixture of oil and butter. Chill a bottle of Maria's white Bordeaux, cases of which still remained in the lazarette. I could put out about three dinners before reverting to my default setting which was takeout.

Murray said "So you're not telling me that seagull you rescued was really a Mexican witch?"

"I didn't say that."

"Hey, you rescued an animal in distress. You should get a commendation from the SPCA. You know, Charlton Heston."

"That's guns."

"Whatever. What did you put on these shrimps?"

"Old family secret."

"Damn good. And you're not saying her mother hired some fortune teller to set your car on fire?

"No, I'm not saying that. I'm trying to tell you the old lady believes in this kind of thing and I think she's getting to Maria."

"Yeah. I can understand that. She goes back there every night after work. They spend a lot of time together. It's natural. You don't believe any of that crap, do you?"

I poured him another glass of white Bordeaux. "It doesn't matter. I want her to come back, that's all."

"You get her ass out of a jam up in Lompoc, maybe the rest of this stuff will go away."

"I'm hoping." I ate papaya and shrimp, drank wine. It wasn't bad.

I said "Hey, are you still connected back East?"

He looked up toward the salon headliner. "Probably there's a few numbers I could call. Sooner or later I might get to somebody. I dunno. I've been off the scene for a while."

"Ok, here's the deal. Cossi used to run Santa Barbara. I want to know what happened up there after he died."

"You're talking about the Italian up in Santa Barbara, the one they ran over with the bulldozer?"

144

"They ran him over?"

"Hey, forget it. We're eating." A pause. "This is whitefish?"

"Catfish."

"Fabulous. How did you get it so crisp?"

"Panko."

"You're welcome." He paused. "Ok," he settled back into his chair, "you want some advice on this thing you got into up north?"

"You bet."

"Ok. First of all, you got boats and crooks? Someone's going to be smuggling something. What happens, it's what that lady told you on the boat. It's just like during Prohibition, you gotta get the stuff off the big boat, then onta the little boat, then on the street. Some things never change. When I left the City it was drugs, before that it was bootleg booze. Before my time. Now, they bring in a load and drop it in the water where it's not too deep, then later on someone else can come along in another boat and pick it up. They would put some gadget on it with a battery, so you'd know where it is."

He started patting his jacket pocket for a cigar, so we went back to the aft cockpit for ventilation.

Ducks spotted us at the rail and paddled over for a handout. Every time Murray flicked cigar ash in the water they went for it, then looked up at us reproachfully. After a few tries they learned cigar ashes didn't taste good.

Murray said "You mind if I call New York from your phone, maybe Boston? Probably I can find out what you want to know. It may take a while. Whoever calls me back, he's gotta go find a boot."

"Boot?"

"Yeah, a phone boot."

A half-hour later Murray returned to the aft cockpit and sat in one of the two teak folding chairs I keep there, put his feet up on the transom.

He said "I got the noise from George the Giant, old friend

of mine. He was a guest at my Bar Mitzvah, that's how far back we go." He had a fresh, unlit cigar in his hand. "We went into the rackets together. He was big even then, six foot six, biggest Yid I ever saw. Now he's got a joint on Flatbush Avenue, a luncheonette, and he's tight with Frank Evangelisti."

"Who's that?"

"The Pope."

"Oh."

"The Pope of Brooklyn, not the real Pope."

"Of course."

"Anyway, George always wanted to move out to the Coast, so Evangelisti got him connected in Santa Barbara but it didn't work; they made fun of him 'cause he's a giant with a Brooklyn accent so thick you could spread it on a bagel. Back home, nobody noticed. Everybody talks like that. So he hadda go back to the City, but he fuckin' hates them. You ask him, he'll talk for an hour. He says Cossi was in charge of Santa Barbara. The story is Cossi got too frisky, first with the construction equipment, then with his sources."

"What sources?"

"George says whatever drugs went out on the street in Santa Barbara was supposed to come from Los Angeles, but Cossi was getting it cheaper someplace else, and was saving tons of money, and when Los Angeles wanted a piece he told them to fuck off."

I remembered what Vic Cannizzarro did to the lobster.

Murray said "That, and stealing the bulldozers and stuff after he was asked not to." He shrugged.

I said "So who's in charge up there now?"

"George says nobody important is actually on the scene. They got the street action, you know what I mean, drugs, some gambling. They had to stop with the hookers, there's a couple of restaurants and the wholesale fish business, that's it. They're letting Cossi's widow keep most of the Lincoln dealership. Every week or so someone comes up from LA to see that everything's running right, drop things off, pick things up, whatever." He looked over the rail at the murky waters of C Basin. "You got anything we could feed these ducks?"

"They don't like cigar ashes."

"And this is a fine cubano, too. Maybe some old bread."

I went forward and returned with half a loaf that had come back in the camper from Lompoc. He started breaking it up into small chunks and throwing them in the water, which soon attracted a dozen or so ducks. Then some seagulls that swooped overhead and dived for the floating bread, confounding the ducks.

Murray said "It's not hard to figure when you two went down to that beach at night, you busted up somebody's little party. Mostly, people don't take guns to the beach."

"Maria did."

He sighed. "I told you before, Tommy, and God forbid I should hurt anybody's feelin's, but you got a gal there, she shoots guns, she rides motorcycles, what kind of a lady does that?"

"You told me one day she was going to shoot me in the middle of an argument."

"I said that?"

"Sort of."

"Don't tell her, ok?"

"She would laugh. She likes you."

"Ok, so we got her on the beach, armed, we got you there, and more people with guns. So it's easy to figure out; if they're bringing in dope, they don't want company."

"Now tell me why my old buddy in the US Attorney's Office had a picture of me driving that fucking SUV across the border?"

"It was you, huh?"

"No doubt about it."

"And he paid for dinner?"

"Yeah."

"He wants something."

"I told you, he threatened me. He was telling me

147

something about Santa Barbara but he didn't want to spell it out. He told me to stay away from Santa Barbara. I think he wants Maria's lawyer to plead it down and tell her to take a dive."

Murray looked doubtful. "Cop to what? There's a dead body, isn't there?"

"Not exactly. There was blood on the sand the morning after. The dead body washed in the next day."

"The dead body washed in?" He walked to the railing and a crowd of ducks zoomed toward him like paparazzi. We were out of stale bread.

Murray said "They match the blood with the body?"

"Nobody told me."

"So she's supposed to plead to what?"

"I can't imagine. But they don't want her to go to trial."

Murray looked thoughtful. "Could only be... could only be they've got their own guy in there."

"In where?"

"Santa Barbara." His eyes brightened. These were challenges retirement didn't offer him. "Look," he went on, "If Cossi's people are bringing drugs in from TJ, how come your guy's got a picture of it? He didn't find that in a Crackerjack box."

"So?"

"So it's his dope your buddy Larry is bringing up to his own undercover guys." He paused. "So on the beach that night we got real hoodlums, the undercover guys, the credit card guy, and you two little lovebirds. And you know what?"

"What?"

"I am prepared to offer very attractive odds that the shooting they're trying to pin on your lady was done by an undercover cop."

28

Al Frankenstein bought me a Jag at the car auction without being asked. I think it helped that he was bucks ahead on the burned-out Toyota. In any case he found a nice-looking blue 1999 XJ6 with high miles but a strong engine. He was going to give it to me for his price, which was very reasonable, but something happened. A rat gave birth in it. And that was the good news.

I drove the Jag for two days. On the morning of the third day it wouldn't start. The man from Auto Club showed up in the parking lot at the Marina and popped the hood. On a flat spot on top of the engine there was a collection of wispy, burned-looking bits of grass and a few twigs, surrounding a number of little cooked rat babies. It took us a while to figure out what they were. It was not uncommon, I was told, for rats to invade cars and make various kinds of mischief inside, but it was a new experience for me and I found it impossible to get

149

the image out of my mind. We're not exactly talking Bambi's mother here, but they were babies, and I had apparently done the deed. Was it witchcraft? The story was too weird to tell Al Frankenstein. When I returned the Jag I told him the car didn't feel right. He looked hurt. I took a cab to the office.

The kid in the wheelchair and the black man with the gray hair were there waiting for me. For a moment I'm thinking, cooking class? Little workshop groups between class meetings, like we used to do in standup comedy workshops? We're going to re-do the lamb loin at home? And who figured out where to find me?

There had apparently been words between them and Marilyn our receptionist. She sat at her desk stoically, eyes front, telephone in hand, no doubt attempting to reach me. I remembered I had left my cell phone behind in the Jag and wondered if rats had gotten to it. If only.

Marilyn said "They're not in the appointment book."

I looked at the two of them and said "Go away." No luck. The black man had shed the camo jacket for a black silk sports shirt, black denim jeans and the kind of ostrich-skin boots prized by very wealthy cowboys. Skinny still looked like he needed a sandwich. Different flannel shirt; same blanket. They were both making a serious effort to look mean. I figured the kid for a gun under the blanket. I mean, it's an ideal place for one; why not? The black man's muscles were packed into his shirt so tightly he couldn't have concealed a bus transfer. But then he didn't need a gun, did he?

I said "Well, what a surprise. Tell me, did you ever try to do the lamb loin?"

They both said 'what?' at the same time, and looked confused."

I said "Cooking class. You don't remember?"

The black man said "Fuck that shit," which caused Marilyn to get up from her position behind the reception desk and disappear into the suite. I doubted she would return to work after that. Now these two knuckleheads owed me a good receptionist.

Skinny said "We're with Homeland Security."

I said "That's nice. I'm Condoleezza Rice."

Skinny looked blank. Maybe he didn't follow politics. The black man said "We want to help you stay out of trouble."

I said "If you guys are from the Government you should be able to show me some identification."

Skinny smiled. "It's secret," he said.

His buddy said "Homeland Security," drawing it out in the way that someone else might have said 'praise the Lord.' Then he said "Where's your girlfriend?"

Skinny said "We saw you on the dock in Santa Barbara last week. You should stay away from there."

He looked over at Homeland, who stirred in his chair, probably suppressing a wish to crush me like a bug. I prayed they had not associated me with Ted and Debbie DeSantis, or the vessel *Katie.*

Homeland got up and walked over to where I was standing, until he was only inches away. He said "You know, while you're standing here being a smartass that cunt girlfriend of yours could be having an accident on her motorcycle."

It put me into an overdrive I didn't know I had. I grabbed the lapels of his silk shirt, lowered my head and pulled him violently toward me, butting him in the nose with my head. At the same time I attempted to knee him in the crotch, which didn't seem to go so well, as he had thighs like tree trunks and I thought my knee might have bounced off muscle before reaching its target.

This is a bar fighting technique. I learned it from an Australian client who had been arrested and charged with mayhem for performing this trick in a bar in Santa Monica. He had demonstrated the technique with me in the office, very gently, then I sat in court at the prelim and watched a deputy city attorney and her assistant demonstrate it for the Judge. It never occurred to me that I might use the head-butt maneuver myself one day. If done suddenly enough, it will completely

151

incapacitate any opponent, even one who could have slowly and carefully beaten you to death, given the chance.

This time it worked spectacularly. Homeland Security now lay on my reception room rug bleeding copiously from his nose. He had assumed the fetal position with one hand at his groin and the other at his face. My knee had evidently reached its target despite the tree trunk thighs protecting his precious parts.

My hands were shaking badly. It took me four tries to punch in 911. Skinny had not moved the whole time.

Then he said "You're not going to hurt him any more, are you?" I said I would not. "Ok, he said. "I'm leaving. Tell the paramedics he fell. He'll back you up. You, however, are now in deep shit. You have no idea what you've just done." And he wheeled his way out the door to the elevator lobby and was gone. I sat in a chair in the reception area, trying to calm down while watching the big man bleed on my rug. Lawyers and secretaries crowded the inner doorway. Nobody wanted to enter the reception area and I didn't feel like chatting. By the time the paramedics arrived I was able to utter the words "He fell," but from the skeptical looks this statement evoked I might as well have said he flew in the window. But it was all I would say, and sooner or later they stopped asking me questions and carted my smashed-up visitor off to the ER.

I took a Xanax and put my feet up on my desk. I refused to take calls, including one from Larry Hayden who, my secretary Phoebe said, had cursed and screamed when she told him I was in conference. She said "You don't want to know what he called you." I had no idea what had gotten his tits in a tangle. He should have been here.

29

"*O la. Señorita Zaragoza, con permiso.*"
"*Que?*"
"*Señorita Zaragoza. Es muy importante. Señor Gomez aqui.*"

It sounded like Maria's assistant Shelly Bustamante. She started to giggle and said "*Momentito Señor Gomez,*" and put me on hold.

Maria picked up. She was giggling too. It's amazing what you can do with a little tomfoolery.

"Tom," she said, "when are you going to drop the *Señor Gomez* routine? You crack Shelly up every time."

"So I bring a note of humor into your life. Is that so bad? Anyway, I do the *Señor Gomez* act because you won't take my calls."

"Wrong. I do not take your calls because I am in a meeting or out in the field. What I do is not return your calls. And this is because my lawyer has told me not to talk with you and because the County is going broke and discourages its employees from making personal calls at work."

153

"You could call from home."

"Fat chance. She keeps the phone locked in a drawer. She believes bad things can come out of it."

"She's right. Come back to the boat and I'll let you make all the calls you want; eat food, drink wine, have sex."

"Simultaneously?"

"Sure. Why not? I even had a Jag for a few days. I could have given you a ride in it, but it's gone."

"What do you mean? Did you have an accident?"

"In a way. A mommy rat had her babies in it."

"What?"

I related to her the short unhappy history of the rat family. She was silent for a few moments and I could hear Shelly talking on the phone in the background. Then she said "You cooked them?"

"In a manner of speaking. I didn't know they were there."

"And you drove around with them?"

"Not for long. I brought the car back to Al's lot as soon as I found out what happened."

"With the dead rat babies inside?"

"No. I cleaned them out with a whisk broom. Actually, I didn't want Al to know. You know, first I get the Volvo soaked at a car wash, then the Toyota burns down on the freeway. I didn't want him to get the wrong idea."

"You mean the right idea."

"Huh?"

"Never mind. What else is new?"

I related my encounter with Wheelchair Jack and Homeland Security, anticipating praise. When I had finished there was a pause, then she said "I see."

"You see? That's all you've got to say? You sound like Lee Brown. You hadda be there to see this mass of muscle lying there in a pool of blood as big as Lake Superior."

"You sound pleased with yourself."

"Well, when you consider the only physical skills I've ever learned are boat driving and how to play the clarinet badly."

154

"And now you can smash noses."

"Right." It's true; I was pleased with myself.

"But who exactly was he?"

"Well, I saw him first in cooking class."

"You beat up a student from cooking class?"

"Not exactly. Don't get excited. It turned out he was part of Cossi's Santa Barbara crew."

"Oh, now I see. You beat up somebody in the Mafia, but I shouldn't get excited. Jesus, Tom, they'll kill you. What's come over you?"

"He called you a cunt and told me you might have an accident on your motorcycle."

"Which you fixed by smashing his nose and rupturing his testicles."

"I'm not sure about the testicles."

"Tom..." Her tone of voice changed. "The boat's a mess, right?"

"Well, it's not up to your standards."

"Galley full of dirty dishes?"

"It's not full."

"No one's done the laundry?"

"I did some socks."

"Ok. You know my brother Domingo's kids Marta and Estrella?"

"Yeah. They run a house cleaning service, don't they?"

"I'm sending them down to the boat tomorrow. You going to be in the office?"

"I'll be up north all day. Does this mean you're going to come back?"

"Maybe not right away, but meanwhile I want to keep you healthy."

*   *   *

"Please state your full name for the record."

"Thomas Merton McGuire."

155

"What is your occupation?"

"I'm a lawyer."

"Where do you reside?"

"Marina del Rey, California."

"And you practice law there?"

"Yes, I do."

"You live on a boat, do you not?"

"What's that got to do with it?"

"Do you know Miss Maria Zaragoza?"

"Yes."

"How would you characterize your relationship with Miss Zaragoza?"

"Friendly."

"Do you have an intimate relationship with Miss Zaragoza?"

"Not lately."

"Mr. McGuire, could you please relate to the Grand Jury the circumstances that led to your presence at Point Sal Beach State Park on the evening in question?"

"Mr. Prosecutor, at this point I must respectfully decline to answer any further questions and assert my right against self-incrimination under the Fifth Amendment to the United States Constitution."

"Thank you, Mr. McGuire. You may step down."

30

On the way back to town my cell phone squealed. It was a replacement for the one that went away with the Jag, and it made a kind of dying-hamster noise when a call came in. Remember when they used to ring?

Lee said "You fived it?"

"Yep."

"I sent you copies of all the discovery I got from the Prosecutor. You should get a lawyer."

"I am a lawyer."

"With a fool for a client."

"I had to assume they'd have Mahmoud's files. I can't get up on the stand and explain the pictures he took of me taking mail out of a drop behind a carwash in Boyle Heights. The mailbox had my name on it and it was the address used to get the credit card that bought the Lincoln. How am I going to explain that to the Grand Jury? And who would believe it? It was addressed to me but it wasn't really my mail; I was stealing it?"

"You could have helped us, Tom. You could have testified she didn't go out with the gun, she didn't argue with anyone, you couldn't have seen squat for the fog. They've got witnesses. You're the only one on our side. You want me to put her on the stand?"

So much for Lee's high standards. I said "You're the one who told me there was a conflict of interest, now you're giving me advice? What if I don't get indicted after all? It could happen. Then I just keep taking the Fifth if anybody asks questions."

"And leave Maria to twist in the wind?"

"I really don't like that image, Lee."

"Sorry. You know what I mean."

"If I have to go in the tank to help Maria I'll do it."

"At trial?"

"Of course. I'd take the rap and go to jail for her if I had to."

"Don't get carried away."

"That happened when I fell in love with her."

That stopped Lee for a while, and I continued down Highway 1 with my cell phone at my ear, beginning to get a cramp in my arm.

Lee said "Well, they're going to prosecute Maria with you or without you. The DA thinks you two conspired to kill Mahmoud in order to conceal a credit card fraud. Not much happens in Santa Barbara County except for Michael Jackson, and that was a while ago. They want a big murder trial."

"You sound like you can't wait."

*   *   *

Den Mother was cleaner than she had been in weeks. The

galley sparkled. Refrigerator defrosted. Old newspapers had been thrown away and magazines stacked. There was evidence of a through vacuuming. Bathroom fixtures had been polished, beds made, my prize Kazakhstan carpet beaten and replaced in the salon. There was a slight smell of an unusual perfume in the air.

On the main transverse bulkhead running amidships between the salon and the aft quarters I noticed the kids had hung a small mahogany crucifix between the ship's clock and the barometer. Not something I would have expected, but I figured their customers were likely to be Hispanic, and therefore Catholic, and would probably like to be surprised by such a gift; a new blessing on a newly cleaned home.

It reminded me of my father, who, I had been told, had been passionate about the Church in his youth, even considering becoming a priest, until he outgrew his adolescence and decided he wanted to keep company with a Jewish girl, a person who would later become my mother. The way I heard the story as a small boy, his family turned on him like a herd of enraged Catholic elephants, the priest leading the charge. Masses were said for him, individual prayers offered, blessings extended, and when they didn't appear to be working, curses uttered. They would have hung him upside down by his heels from the church steeple on Sunday, had the law allowed it. This was the Bronx of a long time ago, and *West Side Story* would not get written and produced for many years. *Abie's Irish Rose* wasn't even a memory.

Not surprisingly, it soured Pop on the Catholic Church. The priest refused to marry them. So did the rabbi. After the marriage (which took place at City Hall) my father stopped going to Mass. He spent his Sundays playing golf with the officers of the labor unions he represented in court during the week. They were mostly Jewish, and had their Sundays free. It was the end of Catholicism as he knew it, although some years later, when I was a small boy, he unaccountably tried to inflict the whole business on me.

I figured I'd leave the crucifix where it was until Maria returned, and see what happened. Then I found another one hanging in the galley, and once I started looking, a total of six.

I didn't like the picture of a saint I found hanging over my bed in the aft stateroom. When I was growing up in New York City these luridly colored religious lithographs could be found for sale in Puerto Rican neighborhoods. I had never seen one up close. This one depicted a woman in a veil and shawl, against a black background, arms outstretched, with a representation of a halo around her head. Sometimes you can tell which saint it is by what they're doing in the picture. Saint Sebastian, for example, is usually shown shot full of arrows. This one was unfamiliar, so I read the inscription at the bottom. It read *'La Santisima Muerte.'* The dead saint? The saint of death? Then I noticed that beneath the halo was a skull, not a face. The dead saint. I didn't recognize this figure from my force-fed exposure to Catholicism. It was creepy. I didn't just take it down, I put it out in the dock box. Why take chances?

I found a business card the cleaners had left behind. It stated that both 'traditional' and 'modern' cleaning services were offered. I thought it would be a good idea to have a telephone conversation with Estrella.

The 'traditional' cleaning services were spiritual, as I had supposed. She told me it was possible *Den Mother* was *enbrujado*, hexed, or bewitched if you prefer, although she had never been on a boat before and couldn't be sure. Both she and her sister had the *don* to some extent, she said, the gift of *curanderismo*, and many of their Hispanic customers sought them out for this reason. When you buy a house that others have lived in, she explained to me, you don't want to deal with the energies they left behind. What if there had been great suffering, she asked me? What if there had been a death? I offered no argument.

Then I remembered Maria telling me that she was sending Marta and Estrella down to the boat because she wanted to keep me healthy. I had wondered about it at the time. What had she asked them to do for me? I asked Estrella this, but here things got vague. The boat felt bad, she said. Maria had told them to clean it thoroughly, and they had. They had left behind the crucifixes. We always leave those, she said. There had been some incense used, and some perfume. I told her my objections to *La Santisima Muerte*, and what had become of her picture. There was a silence.

"Do not leave her in the box outside," Estrella said "*Muy peligroso.*" Very dangerous. Then she told me to take the picture that had upset me so much, remove it from its frame and wrap it up with a picture of the boat, a picture of me, and one of the crucifixes they left behind. Tie it up with twine, she said, and hide it somewhere on board. To my amazement I heard myself tell her that I would do this.

Later, I noticed that the cleaning service, be it 'traditional' or 'modern,' had extended to combing the accumulation of hair out of my hairbrush. Where was my hair? I remembered something about this from an article I'd read about voodoo, and I started rethinking the whole business.

I called Maria at work. "*Señor* Gomez is dead," I told Shelly Bustamante, "and I am calling to invite *Señorita* Zaragoza to the funeral."

She recognized my voice, and the message upset her enough to get Maria on the line.

"What now?" She said. I didn't recognize her voice, and thought for a moment it was Shelly.

"What is your mother doing to me?"

A long silence. I heard background noises and wondered whether they still used typewriters at Adult Protective Services.

"You frightened Shelly," she said.

"You wouldn't have taken the call."

"I'm working, Tom. This is the only piece of mind I have. My cases."

"You sent the girls down to the boat to protect me from your mother and her, what did you call them?" I didn't want to say 'witches.'

"Did they clean the boat?"

"Sure."

"Do the dishes and the laundry?"

"Yeah, and the rugs, and they polished the-"

"-so forget about my mother."

"Come back."

"No."

"At least have dinner with me." I was pleading, and I knew it. What were my choices?

"Tom, listen to me." There was something in her voice I had never heard before. "I'm about to lose my job. I've never been in trouble like this before. I need to be at home. It hasn't been the same since Pop died. She's not like she used to be. She says strange things to me. She's furious at you, she's furious at me. She's had visitors coming and going; people I've never seen before. If I see you, she'll know."

"How? By magic?"

"Tom, you are such an idiot." She was crying now. She broke the connection.

31

I looked over the files Lee had sent me. Photographs of blood on the sand, of bullet holes in the Lincoln, of bullet holes in Mr. Mahmoud, whose files the DA had indeed acquired, complete with the photographs I had seen the investigator taking of my mailbox theft behind Mendoza's Modern Car Wash. Before I had a chance to get too mad at Mr. Mahmoud I read the autopsy report. Massive trauma, multiple gunshot wounds. No slugs to match with a murder weapon. DNA sent out for analysis and not back yet. Then I read the witness statements, which motivated me to call Lee Brown.

"There's only one witness that nails her, Lee."

"Right. Mr. Cabral."

"Bobby."

"You know him?"

"Not exactly. Let me ask you something. Do they have

any case left without this witness?"

"Zilch, really. They can show that you two might have had a motive because of the fraud investigation, but without the witness there's nobody to connect Maria with any actual conduct on the beach that night. He's the one who said she was arguing with the vic; he's the one who puts her next to the Lincoln with a gun in her hand. He says he saw her shoot him."

"Yeah. In the fog."

"Guy's got x-ray vision. What can I tell you? He says it was a light mist. He could see everything."

"So without Mr.Cabral...?"

"I told you, zilch, nada, but what difference does it make? Is Cabral going to take a long vacation?"

"Maybe so."

"I don't want to hear about it."

"Suit yourself. What about this picture of the Lincoln?"

"Which one?"

"One of the pictures the DA produced. There's a shot of the SUV outdoors in front of a chain link fence."

"Yeah. That's in the impound yard. It's locked up tight."

"They've got it outside? Aren't they afraid something might happen to it?"

"Like what?"

*   *   *

Vic Cannizzarro was expounding upon the virtues of chicken.

"To the cook," he said "chicken is like the blank canvas to an artist." A direct steal from Brillat-Savarin. I had the book.

He proceeded to demonstrate stuffed chicken breasts three ways, going from broccoli and pesto-cream sauce to sweet sausage, and ending with prosciutto and Madeira. Everyone got a little serving of each one.

I had come mostly to see who turned out and to have a conversation with Vic after the show, so I didn't pay much

165

attention to the stuffed chicken breasts. The crowd was good, but none of the exotics had turned out tonight; no wiseguys, no FBI that I noticed, no Homey or Wheelchair Jack. Just good solid well-dressed Brentwood Ladies.

On a break Vic motioned me over and I stood with him behind the demonstration table.

He said "You busted up a guy who's friends of some friends of ours."

"You bet I did. He called Maria a cunt and threatened her; said she might have a motorcycle accident."

"He called her a cunt?" He looked grave. "I'm not gonna take sides here, but all those dumb fucks who ride motorcycles have accidents sooner or later. No offense to your girlfriend." He found a stray slice of prosciutto on the table and ate it. "Anyway," he continued, "it was your lucky day. The people I'm telling you about, Lou took your side. Don't ask me. I hadda tell them to let you be. Maybe the guy you messed up shouldn'ta leaned on you like he did. What'd you do to him?"

I explained the head-butt and knee-to-groin trick.

Vic whistled softly. "They teach you that in law school?"

"Yeah. There's a special class in how to beat up clients."

"It's not funny. Now I owe my friends a favor."

"And I owe you one. So let me pay you back."

"Huh?"

"Last week there was a guy here in a wheelchair."

"I didn' notice."

"Yeah, well, he was here with the guy I, uh, injured."

"So?"

"So the guy in the wheelchair is in the wholesale fish business in Santa Barbara, and he gets a lot of his stuff from a guy named Bobby Cabral."

Vic looked at his watch. "Listen, break's over. I gotta get back to work. You got something to tell me, say it." He turned his back on me and started rummaging in a small refrigerator under the demonstration table.

"What I want to tell you is Bobby Cabral's gone in

166

business for himself. Nobody's watching him, and some of what he's hauling out of the water is going in his pocket. He can do better selling to his own customers."

Cannizzarro measured out several cups of heavy cream into a bowl on the table and selected a whisk. He said "Now you're in the fish business?"

"Take it or leave it, Vic. I'm up there all the time. Been going for years. I know lots of commercial fishermen. You think there are any secrets on the waterfront?"

"I wouldn't know." He turned to look at me. "Excuse me, Tom, I gotta make cannolli."

*   *   *

I figured it for a week but it only took them three days to drown Bobby Cabral and burn his boat. The story appeared in the *Santa Barbara News-Press*, which I had taken to reading. Water in his lungs, no marks on his body, boat burned to the waterline. Evidently even diesel-powered craft are subject to catastrophic fires. A dangerous business, fishing.

I couldn't decide whether to be elated or appalled. I felt like a stage magician who had just sawed a woman in half for real. There's no question things like that are more fun when they're illusions.

I had to tell somebody so I stopped off and told Murray on my way to work. We stood on the dock next to his boat as he read the newspaper story. Me in a suit and tie, Murray in faded cut-offs and a pink and red aloha shirt with a pattern of crabs, shrimp and lobsters.

He finished reading and looked thoughtful. "They didn't do this just cause a what you told that guy. Anyone can make up a story like that."

I said "You told me how to do it."

"I told you?"

"You said you just have to remember how things used to be."

167

"So?"

"So they've got this kid pulling crab pots full of drugs. He's supposed to deliver the stuff to Wheelchair Jack. A friend of mine in Santa Barbara told me Jack's buddy, a black guy they call Homeland Security, used to go out on Bobby's boat with him."

"To make sure he didn't steal from the company?"

"What else? Now, remember what I told you I did to this Homeland guy?"

"You busted his beezer."

"His balls, too, I'm hoping."

"Good on you. So he doesn't feel like going out on the water for a while, and meantime the kid dips his hand in the product? That's what you figured?"

"That's what they figured, right?"

Murray looked thoughtful. "Damn. That's what I would have figured, too. The runner will always steal product." He laughed. "Back in the city we had a guy doin that to us with numbers bets. A runner. He'd just shitcan enough of them to make a little cash on the side. None of the schmucks that bet the numbers ever won more than a few bucks, so mox nix, right? Once in a while he'd have to pay somebody off. So finally one of the numbers this guy stole paid off big and he had to kill the guy who made the bet to keep it quiet. That's how he got caught."

"Your people didn't know he was stealing?"

"No, but like you said, if somebody had told us 'watch out for this guy, he's shitcanning numbers bets,' we'd a caught him easy." He gave me a long look. "Y'know, I'm lookin at you, nice suit, nice tie, shoes all shined. Even got yourself a manicure, dincha?" I nodded. Maria had suggested it. "And you're playing in the street. A choirboy." He shook his head.

"I was never a choirboy."

"Up until now ya coulda fooled me."

32

Lee Brown's phone message was 'thanks for a job well done,' and an invitation to lunch at the restaurant on the ground floor of his office building in Westwood. He was sitting at a corner table when I arrived, looking at a small salad. I had never seen him eat anything other than a small salad, nor drink any alcohol.

Lee projected an odd mixture of scholar and soldier; the look of a big-ticket criminal lawyer, with just a hint of the kind of innocent-looking young kid who would not be above playing a nasty trick on someone. I thought of him as a friend, but I had absolutely no idea what went on inside his head.

I sat down, and when a waiter arrived ordered a strip steak medium rare, fries and a beer. Lead by example is my motto.

169

"So," I said, "thanks for what?"

He looked up from his salad. "It's over. They've got no case. The only charges they could go with now would be based on the gun, which is chickenshit and they couldn't prove it anyway."

"You mean like keeping a loaded firearm in a motor vehicle?"

"Yeah. They get pissed at civilians who turn up armed, under any circumstances."

"Right. People who could maybe shoot back."

"That's the idea. They want to be able to do all the shooting." He poked at his salad with a fork as though he thought something might be hiding in it.

I said "So how was this my doing?"

My meal arrived. Lee looked at it, then looked away.

"Bobby Cabral," he said. "Their only witness. When he turned up dead they had nothing they could bring to trial."

I looked around the mock-Tudor restaurant, pretty much full now with a lunchtime crowd. Well turned-out West Side types, at least six of whom were close enough to our table to be able to overhear our conversation.

"That's what you're thanking me for?"

Lee ate a bite of salad and raised an eyebrow. Oh, the ponderous irony of the legal profession, the snickers and winks, the whole superior in-crowd we-know-better act. Except this time it was no joke. Did he somehow know?

"Just a joke, Tom. Don't look so stricken." He paused, looked worried. "You shouldn't eat such heavy food at lunchtime."

"I hate people telling me what to eat."

That put the kibosh on conversation for a while. I had lost my appetite. Lee thought he had hurt my feelings, but I didn't like to think about my role in Bobby Cabral's death. And I sure as hell didn't want to be thanked for it.

He said "It worked out perfectly. I've been well paid, and now I don't have to try the case. Don't even have to plea-

170

bargain. I'm a hero. It's funny, really. Every time I've got a case where a witness dies or disappears, people think I had something to do with it."

"Maria paid you?"

"I think it came from her mother."

"You're not going to give some of it back?"

"Why? Look at the result. No plea deal, no trial, no nothing; she'll walk on water. You don't think that was worth it?"

"But you just said I was responsible for the result."

"So, you want some of the fee?"

"Hell no."

"Don't get excited."

Some of the nearby diners were looking over at us. I couldn't help it; now Lee was going to pay me for taking Bobby Cabral out of his case. Perfect!

Lee said "I did do something for you. I got a Motion granted releasing some of the property they took."

"What property?"

"Well, for openers, not the .357 Magnum. The Judge let them keep it for awhile." He laughed. "Judges hate guns, and it was what she really wanted. She cares a lot about her guns, doesn't she?"

"Like a little girl cares about her dolls."

He gave me a look. "So they get to keep the gun, but they've got to give us back the car."

"What car?"

"The Lincoln Navigator."

"What?"

"Quiet down, Tom. Please, I eat here a lot. The car, SUV, whatever the hell you call it. They've got to release it."

"To who?"

"That's where I helped you out." He produced an envelope from his jacket pocket and handed it to me. "Y'see, I don't represent you, so I can't ask the Court to release the Lincoln to my client. That's how this type of Motion is usually

171

phrased. You know, give my guy back his property. And it's kind of complicated, between you and the credit card company, so I drafted it so it said they have to give back the car to its owner, upon satisfactory proof of ownership. Sounds right, doesn't it? Except if it doesn't belong to my client why am I asking them to give it back? I doubt the Judge even read it. He signed the Order."

"So what?"

"You don't want it back?"

I took a deep breath. "Lee, I don't think you've been following this too closely. It's not mine. I only drove it once, and so far it's done a good job of destroying my life."

"All by itself?"

He looked interested, which was unusual for Lee. I thought back to the morning I got the call from MasterCard; the call I thought was a rattlesnake, the revenge I was going to exact.

I said "It's hard to explain."

Lee let the waiter take away his salad. He ordered a cup of coffee and looked at his watch.

"Never mind, " he said. "I figured somebody might want the damn thing so I stuck it in. She asked me to get the gun back, so I had to do the Motion anyway. You don't want the Lincoln, forget it. It'll sit in an impound up in Lompoc until somebody figures it out." He looked around for his coffee. "I gotta get back to work."

I sat alone and looked at the remains of my steak, ordered another beer. I had dropped a dime on Bobby Cabral to protect Maria, and somebody had killed him. By protecting her, I had upset somebody else's plans. I wasn't exactly sure whose, but it wasn't long before I found out.

33

I was eating sushi across the street from my office when Murray called me on the cell phone and told me I had problems at home.

"There's four guys in suits," he said, "sitting on your dockstep looking hostile. There's two more in a plainclothes car in the parking lot."

"There's only three steps on my dockstep. It must be crowded."

"So maybe one guy's sitting in another guy's lap. Get serious, fachrissakes."

"You going to be on board for a while?"

"Yeah."

"I'll call you right back."

I called the office and learned there were two more

174

hostile guys in suits in my reception area, unhappy that I was not there. And probably two more in the parking lot. Larry's work.

If you've ever been in real danger you'll understand what I did next. There's a point where you can either fall apart or make a series of quick decisions. Right or wrong, you deal them out like cards and act on them without reflecting if you're doing the right thing, without giving yourself time to doubt. Even a bad choice is better than being a deer in the headlights; paralyzed by fear. At least you're still in the game.

I called my secretary on an inside line and told her to gather up all the Lincoln Navigator materials and the evidence Lee Brown had been given by the prosecutor in Santa Barbara, and to messenger it all to Lee's office where I could get it later. Then I called Murray back and told him to drive over to the Marina Center and meet me at the cell phone store.

I bought two new cell phones before Murray arrived, then we drove to my bank where I emptied the general account. I now had two cell phone numbers nobody knew I had, except Murray, who I trusted, eleven thousand dollars in cash, and after I dropped Murray off two blocks down the seawall from his boat I had his near-new burgundy Mercury Marquis with a full tank of gas. Murray hardly complained at all. I gave him a thousand for the use of his car. I think he liked the action.

On some level I had sensed this was coming. After all, Larry Hayden had done it to me once before; plucking me off the sidewalk outside Chinoise on Main after a fat meal we had enjoyed there that I had paid for. I remembered Larry's angry phone call to the office, the call I hadn't taken because I was still coming down from playing nik-nak on Homeland Security's nose. Phoebe said he had been mad at me about something and it worried me that I didn't know what it was. I would learn soon enough; Larry Hayden was trying to arrest me again. This time the stakes were much higher. I remembered Janis Joplin singing that freedom was just another word for nothing left to lose. Drugs, success and Southern Comfort brought that great lady down. Today, Larry Hayden had given me my freedom. In what corner of the future was my destruction stored?

I parked Murray's Marquis on Pacific Coast Highway in front of the airport, and got Larry at his office.

"Where are you, Tom?"

"Escaping."

"Waste of time. Just come down to the Federal Building and I'll take you before a Magistrate myself. Maybe we can get you back out tonight." Still my friend, trying to help me with a difficult situation. He lived in a dream.

"Horsefeathers. What did I do this time?"

At this point a huge passenger jet passed overhead with what felt like inches to spare.

Larry said "What's that noise?"

"Den Mother. I'm firing up her engines."

"Bullshit. I've got four guys sitting on your boat."

"And two in my office, and in both parking lots. I know. What are the charges?'

"Well, we haven't filed anything yet, but we don't have to under the Patriot Act."

"Now I'm a terrorist?"

"Probably not, but you assaulted an officer of the Department of Homeland Security and attempted to prevent him from carrying out his duties. We can hold you indefinitely."

"You're telling me Homeland Security is with Homeland Security?"

"What? Oh, and don't forget the carload of dope. We've got film on that, and the Santa Barbara County Prosecutor has the car. He's going to give it to us when he's finished with it. You're toast. No more fancy restaurants for you."

"You realize what you're doing to yourself?"

"Huh?"

"Without me, you're never going to eat another restaurant meal costing more than seven dollars and fifty cents. You're looking at a lifetime of chicken-fried steak and Alka-Seltzer."

"Have your fun. The man you assaulted is going to need reconstructive surgery to rebuild his nose. People are very angry with you." Another jet went over at this point and all I caught was the end of his next sentence which was "...could be seriously injured while being taken into custody."

"Larry, have you ever met Wheelchair Jack?"

Silence.

"Yeah, you have." It was time to get creative. "Wheelchair Jack and the guy whose nose I smashed are running drug distribution for spaghetti-heads in Santa Barbara. Everyone on the waterfront knows that. You know that. They're working for you. If your people knew about an SUV fulla dope that came into California from Tijuana, why didn't they stop it?"

"What SUV? What dope?"

"Too late, Larry, I taped you at Chinoise. Digital. Anybody can do it now. Twenty-nine ninety-five on the Internet." It's the details that make this kind of lie convincing.

"And Bobby Cabral," I said, "was he one of yours, too?" Silence. "He's dead, you know. Now you're going to have to figure out another way to get your work done."

Later, I wondered whether the hastily improvised concept of the tape recording of our restaurant conversation had succeeded in frightening Larry more than I had intended. Or maybe on some level I had intended to provoke the kind of misjudgments to which his fear would ultimately lead him. Yeah. I had wanted to scare the shit out of him.

Larry started to say something, then stopped. The conversation had lasted almost two minutes according to the LED readout on the cell phone. I remembered that cell phone calls could be traced.

I said "I gotta go. Maybe I'll call you back later. But don't tell me you're going to prosecute me for assaulting a working drug dealer who happens to be an undercover cop, or for helping the Government provide him with drugs to sell, cause that's silly. You're not going to do it."

I terminated the call, cutting him off in mid-threat, and

177

turned off the cell phone. Below me, down the bluff from Pacific Coast Highway, was Santa Monica Bay and Dockweiler State Beach, deserted now during a weekday except for a few people skating on the bike path.

It was two o'clock in the afternoon, and I was on the lam. I wasn't sure what I should be doing. I felt like a character in an action movie, but I knew it couldn't last more than a few days, a week, outside, before I ran out of nerve and couldn't do it any longer. If Larry got me before I could get some traction on the situation, his Patriot friends would lock me in a holding cell in the Federal Building and throw away the key. No, throw away the holding cell. I could wind up at Guantanamo Bay studying the Koran. I needed some time to think.

I took another look down towards the surfline, then drove the few miles down PCH to Manhattan Beach, where I parked. I bought a beach towel, a bathing suit, a portable radio, and a tote.

I changed in a large concrete structure provided for that purpose by the City of Manhattan Beach, and went out on the sand. After a few minutes I went back and bought a bottle of sunblock and a straw hat.

The Dodgers had apparently blown it in season play, and now needed four games to make it as the Wild Card team. Some Dodgers. The sun was warm. I applied sunblock lavishly, and took a Xanax.

I'm better at intuition than logic. It was my intention to relax and let my unconscious sort things out. Instead, I went to sleep.

Later I was awakened by a soft, squeaky rendition of the Toreador's song from Bizet's *Carmen*, as it might be performed by a rat or mouse. One of my new cell phones, muffled by the tote.

Murray sounded rattled: "I just took a cab over to the Center and five minutes later we get cut off by another car and this guy gets into the cab, says he's a friend of yours and wants to know how to get in touch with you. I tell him I have no idea, then we get to the Center and we both get out. He says he'll check with me when I finish shopping. Tom, what the hell is this?"

"Relax." I scanned the beach for potential threats; saw none. An overweight youngish lady in a too-revealing pink bathing suit, with three bratty little kids; two teenage surfers, a boy and a girl, with perfect bodies, perfect tans. Little bastards; didn't they have jobs to go to?

I said "Did this guy look like he worked for the Government?"

Murray snorted. "Not hardly. More service connected, ya know what I mean."

"White cardigan?"

"Yeah."

"Big diamond bracelet?"

"That's him."

"It's ok."

"Yeah?"

"Yeah. You calling another cab to get back to the boat?"

"Of course I am. You've...I mean, my car's in the shop."

"Sorry to hear that. When you get your cab, chances are this guy will get in with you. When that happens, you call me on your cell, and you can put him on the line."

"It's ok?"

"It's ok."

34

"Jesus, Tom, they told me you were on the run."

How had Lou Gizzi got the news that fast? "Murray tell you what happened?"

Lou laughed. "This little bald-headed guy ain't got a thing to say."

"Be nice. He's a good friend of mine."

"I wanted to talk to you for a few days now. You were never around."

"I've been busy."

"Yeah, anyway you were complainin' to me about that car, the SUV?"

"I remember."

"How it coulda happened the way it did?" I heard him giving driving instructions to the cab driver to take the long way. Lou Gizzi had no interest in appearing on the seawall adjacent to my dock. Evidently, he already knew who might be waiting there.

"To be honest with ya," Lou went on, "it bothered me, you thinking I maybe set you up. Cause I didn't."

"So?"

"Here's the deal. Cossi was in charge of Santa Barbara."

"So what's the story?"

The sun was low in the sky and I had sunburned my back where I hadn't been able to apply the sunblock. I would need to do something, go somewhere, when this call was over, and I had no idea what or where.

"Some people think Cossi was working for the opposition and that's why he got hit. It's a rumor. I wouldn't know."

"Uh-huh."

"Anyway, the way the story goes Cossi would steal a car from his dealership once in a while; get somebody to boost one off the lot, but ya see, that's a stolen car. Right away, there are certain disadvantages. Then somebody got the idea to do this credit card scam; find some poor schmuck's credit info and stick the whole thing on him. Then you can use the car for a few weeks and throw it away, or maybe sell it in Mexico or to the Russians. Plus the dealership's got its profit on the sale to the schmuck. Neat, huh?"

"Get to the point."

"Relax. The point is that certain people gave them your name and credit info and told them to do the deal with you as the designated schmuck."

"Certain people?"

"Yeah. Actually, someone you know."

"Oh, shit."

"Sorry."

Larry Hayden had done it to me; tied the Lincoln Navigator to my tail; figured me in advance for the kind of person who would bravely and stupidly follow the problem down a rathole. And what a string of disasters that one

182

malicious act had put in motion; Maria was almost put on trial for murder, she was off the boat, and for the time being out of my life. I couldn't go home or to the office. Charges and imputations of murder, smuggling, fraud, assault and other misconduct fluttered around me like confetti. Magic spells had been placed on me. Vehicles self-destructed under my hands. Rats fried themselves.

My sunburn flared into an enveloping red rage, the kind that makes a roaring sound in your head. I felt an immediate need to go find Larry Hayden and kill him in spectacular circumstances, pick him to pieces with a dull fork, but the plan offered several serious negatives. I needed a shower badly. I had no weapon. I didn't have a change of socks or underwear, soap, a toothbrush. I was a fugitive.

Strong emotion makes it difficult to think clearly. If I had been calmer it might have occurred to me that Lou had known about the Lincoln Navigator business for some time, but chose to tell me about Larry Hayden's hand in the matter only much later. He could have let me in on the joke the first time I visited him at La Cosa Nostra, and saved me huge amounts of trouble, but he didn't. On reflection, the premise that Lou was now trying to help me seemed the least likely explanation of all, but it was the one I believed. I needed help, and there it was.

My hands were shaking. I lay on my beach towel in the cooling late afternoon and tried to compose myself. I called Lee Brown's office and told his secretary what I wanted done with the materials that had been messengered there from my office. Then I called the Venice Public Library and determined they would be open until nine.

I gathered up my gear and returned to the public changing room, where I hoped I would find showers. The changing room was locked. There were showers there, too. I could see them through the bars. The City Fathers had thoughtfully considered that public toilets should remain open. I changed back into my suit in a toilet stall, but there was sand sticking to the sunblock everywhere I had applied it, and everywhere else, and the suit, shirt and tie had spent the afternoon at the beach, rolled up and stuffed in the tote, and looked the worse for it. I itched everywhere. Fully clothed, I now looked like an unemployed office worker who slept outdoors and washed infrequently. But at the moment, that was more or less what I was.

*   *   *

The librarian gave me a look, but the Venice library had become a magnet for transients, and I guess I fit right in. I signed up and spent a half-hour connected to the internet on one of the free computers. It was all I needed. Then I drove the short distance to Westwood and recovered my documents from the security desk in the lobby of Lee Brown's office high-rise.

I drove to Pearl Street in San Gabriel, and parked directly in front of the Zaragoza residence. It was almost dark and street lights were coming on. I immediately became the subject of intense curiosity on the part of a group of men who were standing across the street. I could see them gesturing towards me. Two or three of them were on cell phones. Then they began to drift across Pearl Street in my direction. I punched in the Zaragoza family home number as someone knocked politely on the driver side window. Just as somebody answered the phone I realized I had driven Murray's car into a trap.

"*Bueno. Quien habla?*" It was *Señora* Zaragoza.

"*Señor* Gomez. Don't hang up. I am parked right outside your house and I am in danger. *Peligro.* Look out your window."

The knocking at the driver side window came again, a little louder. This time someone made a gesture suggesting that I roll down the window. They had completely surrounded the car by now. I saw curtains move in a front window of the Zaragoza home. I clutched the cell phone tightly and spoke into it, I don't remember what I said, but *Señora* Zaragoza had evidently put the receiver down to go take a look at me. Finally she was back.

"*Que quieres?*"

"*Señora, per favor.*" But what was I going to ask her to do for me? Come out with her cane and poke Larry's field agents until they ran away? Please come outside and tell these men not to hurt me? "*Peligro,*" I said. It came out as a sort of croak. 'Danger.' It was the best I could do.

I could hear Maria's voice in the background, then I saw the curtains move again. But *Señora* Zaragoza was not buying it. She spoke to me harshly in rapid Spanish and hung up the phone. I had a pretty good idea what was on her mind. Then Maria appeared on the sidewalk next to the car. She was wearing a bathrobe and slippers, with her hair up in a towel. She spoke quietly to the group, smiling and gesturing toward me. They were homeboys, I realized, kids in their twenties; not what I had feared. My mind got the message, and was relieved. My heart did not, and continued to beat too fast.

Maria was holding what looked like one of her smaller stainless steel semi-automatic handguns, but she continued to smile. It was all very low-key. Neighborly. The group began to disburse. The show was over. I unlocked the passenger door and Maria got inside. I could smell her shampoo.

She said "What was your plan if nobody had been home?"

I took a moment to catch my breath. I said "I'm not thinking too clearly. It's been a difficult day."

I told her the story, beginning with lunch at the sushi joint and Murray's phone call and ending with the drive from Lee Brown's office to San Gabriel. She said nothing. It was impossible to read her expression in the semi-darkness.

"Oh, by the way," I said, "I've got a copy of the *Santa Barbara News-Press* here that has a story about Bobby Cabral. Remember that name? Lee told me he was the only witness against you."

"So?"

"He's dead. Drowned." She made a sign of the cross and

185

murmured something in Spanish. I said "There's no case without him. Didn't Lee tell you he died?"

"I think Lee called here. I told him not to call me at the office. Mama tells people I'm not home, and she doesn't tell me about the calls." She looked at me. "All that really happened? Larry Hayden wants to arrest you and you went to sleep on a beach?"

"Your mother was going to leave me out here on the street, wasn't she?"

"Yes she was. She said the Devil could take you."

"That is still a distinct possibility."

"There were two guys here around lunchtime, guys in suits, looking for you."

"What guys?"

"Mama told me. I was downtown, working. They were probably trying to arrest you. Your friend," she made a mouth, "must have decided you would come out here."

"What happened to them?"

"Mama says they parked down the street for a while, where they could see the house, until some of the neighborhood boys explained they were not welcome and should go back where they came from." She took a close look at me, wrinkled her nose. "You really have been playing in the dirt. You smell."

Fear will do that. "I need a shower and a change of clothes."

"You can buy all the clothes you want on the Boulevard, but you'll have to get the shower elsewhere."

"You don't have inside plumbing?"

"Watch your mouth. You bathing in Mama's house would be just a little less of a scandal to her than us making love on her living room rug."

"I doubt I could do that, but I'm willing to try. It's been a long time." And damn if I wasn't actually getting aroused thinking about it, sitting in my filthy suit with sand in my shorts.

Maria did a brief manual inspection. As she leaned

toward me her robe fell open. I couldn't breathe. Only flesh can do this to me. Maria's flesh.

She said "*Pobre Señor chiquito. El no puede salir ha jugar.*"

Señor chiquito, the little man, might not be coming out to play at the moment, but he was making an heroic effort.

"Ok," she said, gesturing toward my rumpled clothes, "let's start by getting rid of some of this hazardous waste. Two blocks down and go right, there's a motel, La Paloma. Two blocks more down the Boulevard you can buy clothing. Probably not the kind you could wear to court."

"It's not a problem right now. I'm a fugitive."

"Right. I forgot."

Across the yard curtains fluttered in the front window of the Zaragoza home. Maria said "I've got to go back inside. Across the street from the motel there's an all-night coffeeshop. I'll try to get there in two hours, OK?"

I said I would be there.

35

When the opportunity came it was so easy I couldn't believe it. Larry was standing tall at the controls of a trawler that looked like the one Bobby Cabral had been using the night he tried to chase us out of the Point Sal anchorage. He was pointing some kind of firearm at me but I already had him lined up in the sights of Ted DeSantis' 30.06 deer rifle. Before Larry could get off a shot I got him clean in the chest twice and blew him out of the cockpit, into the water. After a few moments it was clear from movement in the water and the spreading red stain that sharks were finishing up what I had started. Then Maria appeared. She was naked and in my arms. I was naked too. We made love. It had been a long time and was over too quickly. But as we lay there in a swoon things became confused. The experience of shooting Larry began to shrink like something seen through the wrong end of a telescope. Did I want it badly enough to try to save it? I curled myself more tightly around Maria's warmth. Larry's tumbling corpse winked out like a light and I was aware of being in bed with Maria in my arms, in the motel room I had rented the night before

I pulled the covers over my head, but not before I noticed that the time on the bedside clock-radio was ten a.m. I took another look. Hung neatly against the closet door was Maria's little blue suit; her go-to-work costume. Her shoes and underwear were on the floor, less neatly arranged. My clothing was everywhere.

Señor chiquito had come out to play at last. Right in that moment everything was perfect. This was where I wanted to stay forever. There is nothing more existential than a cheap motel room. Nobody knew we were here. I wasn't even entirely clear where we were, where here was. But it felt safe.

Now I could recollect going shopping, then renting the room, returning with my purchases and taking a shower. Then I must have laid down for a few moments and fallen asleep. I never made it across the street to the coffeeshop to meet Maria. She must have come here when I didn't show, figured out what had happened and gone home. Then she had left her mother's house this morning on the pretext of going to work, but came here instead to get in bed and get her hands on me and *Señor chiquito*.

She stirred slightly and said "You smell a lot better than you did in the car."

"Right now I smell like you."

"Like us."

"Right."

She said "We can't just stay in bed all day."

"Why not? I paid for two nights."

"Well, for one thing it's almost lunchtime and I'm hungry."

I said "We can't eat in the neighborhood. Someone will see us and tell your mother."

190

"Count on it."

"So, I'll bring the car around and we can smuggle you out in the backseat, under a blanket."

"Which we might be able to use later."

"The blanket?"

"Yes."

"Good thinking."

Which is how we wound up eating in a back booth of a *loncheria* just off Mission Drive in Rosemead. Fish tacos, rice, beans, Tecate. Maria in her little blue suit; me in my new khaki pants and white guayabera shirt. I had brought my briefcase of documents from the car; sorting through them as we ate.

I said "These are the papers we got at Santa Barbara Lincoln Mercury, remember?"

"You want to know do I remember dancing naked on the hood of that car?"

"You weren't completely naked."

"It was the best I could do on short notice."

I showed her the Court Order Lee had given me. She looked puzzled.

She said "What good is this?"

"In case I want to drive it."

"Drive the Lincoln? The one we got in TJ?"

"Right."

"*No mames.* You drove it once and look what happened."

"Ok, never mind. Look at this."

I showed her two photos of Larry Hayden I had downloaded from newspaper archives at the Venice Public Library.

"That's Larry, right?"

"Yep."

"Why are you showing this to me?"

"One more picture." I showed her the photo Lee Brown had given me. The one he got from the Santa Barbara County Prosecutor, showing the Lincoln Navigator locked in the evidence compound.

191

Maria said "That's the Lincoln you drove?"

"That's it."

"With the drugs still inside?"

"Probably not."

"So?"

"So I want it to burn down, like the Toyota I got from Al Frankenstein."

"What good would that do?"

"When I told Al the Toyota was on fire he liked it. He said he could cash in on the insurance and make more money than the car was worth."

"So?"

"Same with the Lincoln. It's insured. If it's a total loss the MasterCard people can take the money and there's a problem solved."

"They won't want to prosecute you for fraud?"

"No. They'll have their money. Basically, all they're about is money."

"Even with Mr. Mahmoud dead? Their own employee?"

"They don't think I killed him, and there's no more case against you. They can always hire more fraud investigators."

"That's cold."

"Yeah, I suppose it is. I shouldn't be unfair to the MasterCard people. They may be, what do you call them, compassionate conservatives. I'm really not myself these days. You know, being a fugitive and all. If those Patriot boys catch up with me Larry says I may not make it into custody."

"Don't pout."

"Yeah, I know. Santa Claus is coming to town." I laid out the photos of Larry and the Lincoln side by side. "Here's the plan. See this car? The *curandera* can make it burn. Don't roll your eyes. I've seen it. Your mother paid for it to happen to me. I can pay, too. I'm holding plenty of money."

She had her head in her hands. A waitress removed the congealed remains of our rice and beans.

I said "Wait. There's more. There's Larry."

She spoke through her hands. "You want him burned down too?"

"No. I want his plans to end in disaster. I want his wife to leave him. I want his undercover agents to make mistakes, to turn against him. I want his organization to distrust him. I want him to be demoted, to be fired, to be suspected of crimes. I want his hair and his teeth to fall out, his eyesight to fail."

She had reached over the table and covered my mouth with her hand. People were staring at me. I could feel my pulse pounding.

Maria said "You're hysterical."

"I'm under a lot of strain."

"Two weeks ago you were laughing at my mother and the *curanderos*. Now you believe in them?"

"I don't think so. It's just that if I screw this up now I won't be able to come back and fix things a second time. I've got a pocket full of cash and it's now or never. I saw the Toyota burn. Never had a car catch on fire before. So why not bet some money on it? You're here. You can take me to the people, right? In Ojinaga?"

"No, actually, they're right across the street."

She gestured through the *loncheria* window toward an office suite across the street, upstairs over a dry cleaners. Spanish language signs in the windows indicated that insurance, immigration, real estate and notary services were available. *Hablamos Español*, as if that was necessary, considering that everything else in the window was in Spanish, too.

Maria gave me a cool look. "You expected it to say *Brujeria*, maybe? Witchcraft?" She took a deep breath. "Just promise me one thing."

"What?"

"Whatever happens, don't ever complain to me that you got cheated, ok?"

"Fine."

"And before we do anything we're going to take a walk

around the block and you're going to get a grip."

36

I could hear the pressing machine hissing in the cleaners downstairs. The corridor smelled starchy. At the end of the corridor was a door with a pebble-glass insert on which was lettered 'Alex Miramon' in gold leaf, and a list of the services available within. A buzzer sounded as we entered a combined reception and secretarial area. No secretary or receptionist. Late-fifties office decor, except for a computer on one of the desks. For customers, a vinyl-upholstered living room set in harvest gold; clunky wooden office furniture for staff, film noir venetian blinds covering the broad windows. On the walls, the kind of processed plywood paneling that was supposed to resemble hardwood but looked more like an exotic skin disease. Outside, the busy sounds of traffic on Rosemead Boulevard.

Mr. Miramon appeared from out of his inner office. He

was a big man, elderly and overweight, his tan face deeply seamed. He had white hair worn long in back, and a three-piece bottle-green suit in a style that evoked newsreels of the Truman administration, except for a complex turquoise and silver belt buckle that I didn't think Harry would have favored.

Maria and Miramon had a brief conversation in Spanish, from which I understood only that he seemed to know her mother. Then Maria gestured toward the sofa and told me to wait. They went into the inner office. I sat for what seemed a long time, listening to the pressing machine. It was one-thirty in the afternoon.

I looked through the briefcase for the photographs of Larry and the Lincoln Navigator, found one of my new cell phones, and decided to call Ted and Debbie DeSantis in Santa Barbara. To my surprise they were unlisted, but the Harbormaster wasn't. His office overlooked the water and I got someone there to go down to *Katie* on the commercial dock and tell Debbie to call me.

"Your home number's unlisted?"

She made an exasperated noise. "It didn't use to be. Things have gotten a little nuts up here, the last year or so." She paused.

I said "I read about Bobby Cabral." Why did I bring this up? The one thing I didn't want to talk about.

Debbie said "I was with his mother last night. Did you know her husband was lost at sea ten years ago? Now it's her son. Ted and Bobby's fathers fished together for a while back in the 60's. Accidents like this shake up the whole community."

"It was an accident?"

"Tom." It was a plea to drop the subject.

"I know, but things have gotten a lot worse since I saw you. I'm in a big fat jam. I need to know what's happening on the waterfront."

There was a pause, then she said "OK, ask your questions, but don't ever mention this conversation to Ted, and forget about using *Katie*. Don't even ask to come aboard. Ted

196

doesn't think it was fair of you to get us up to Point Sal without telling us the whole story."

"He's right. I owe you both an apology."

"Get up off your knees, kiddo, you'll wear holes in your pants."

"Bless your heart." I needed more friends like Debbie.

I said "Ok then, who's pulling pots for Wheelchair Jack and Homeland now that Bobby's gone?"

"Homeland?"

"The black guy with the muscles."

"They asked a few people after Bobby died but everyone's too scared of them. Then they were trying to charter a boat."

"For what?"

"The black guy offered Ted five thousand in cash to use *Katie* for three days. Big joke. We can make more than that in a night, and anyway Ted would never let anyone else run his boat."

"What three days was it?"

"Well, it would have started today, and run through Friday, the day after tomorrow. When they're going to launch a missile at Vandenberg. We couldn't have gone out then. Some of our best runs are off limits when there's a launch."

"Isn't that what Bobby Cabral was saying that night at Point Sal?"

"What?"

"That they were going to launch a missile, and we should get out, we were in some sort of prohibited area."

"Right. The Pacific Missile Range. It's a big square on the chart, and the Air Force has boats that patrol before a launch. They'll run you out. Bobby works for them, but most of the time when he tells you to move your boat, it's just a bluff."

"So they didn't charter *Katie*?"

"No."

"Did they get a boat?"

"That's what I heard. There's a trawl skipper on the dock with busted hydraulics; he can't fish till the parts get here.

They took his boat out yesterday, Ted told me, and nobody's seen it since. They're going to have a lot of fun pulling things off the bottom without oil pressure."

"They?"

"The little white guy in the wheelchair and his friend." Debbie couldn't bring herself to say their names. She said "What happened to his nose?"

"I butted him in the face with my forehead."

"Jesus, Mary and Joseph."

The door to Alex Miramon's inner office opened, and Maria beckoned me to come inside.

Debbie said "One thing, Tom."

"What is it?"

"If you come to Santa Barbara?"

"Yes?"

"Don't come near us, ok?"

*   *   *

The inner office looked much like the outer, but without windows. Same exotic plywood skin disease on the walls. Miramon sat behind a bulky once-stylish desk, fake walnut with leather inserts, generously decorated with cigarette burns. On the desk a lit cigar rested in a large brass ashtray made out of an artillery shell. Behind Miramon was an ego wall of certificates and photographs. He had laminated his Marine Corps discharge papers, and had evidently shaken hands with Cesar Chavez, former Mayor Tom Bradley and a number of other, lesser, luminaries. There was a framed letter from the White House, but I couldn't read the signature.

Maria sat across from Miramon. I stood in the doorway. It did not appear that I was going to be asked to sit down. Miramon stared at me with a blank expression, then noticed I was holding a cell phone, and asked me to turn it off. I did as he asked.

He said "I'm sorry, but I'm going to disappoint you."

198

Maria's expression didn't change. This had been explained to her in advance. "I can sell you an insurance policy, or help if you have an immigration problem or want to buy or sell property, but that's it. I don't pull rabbits from hats." He paused. "I know what many of our people believe, Miss Zaragoza's mother, for example. A wonderful person I have known for many years."

It sounded like the beginning of a eulogy. My eyes strayed across the wall of trophies. Could that be a signed photograph of Shirley McLaine?

He said "Our people believe wisdom comes with age, so because I am old I must be smart. Who knows? But I'm smart enough not to take money to do something I can't do." He stood up; we were being excused.

He said "Miss Zaragoza told me you might be having some trouble with Federal authorities." I said nothing. "Well," he continued, "if you communicate with them by telephone don't use one of those." He gestured toward the cell phone I was still holding in my hand. "With some cell phones they can locate you in ninety seconds."

I said "I didn't know that."

"It's new since late last year. Buy the cheap phones they sell in convenience stores, use them a couple of times then throw them away." There were sides to Mr. Miramon I had not realized were there. Now I asked myself, who was he?

I said "Sounds like good advice." Amazing what you can learn in the real estate business.

He shook my hand and surprised me by grinning like a little boy up to mischief. He may have winked at me. He would not, it seemed, settle down and be any one person in particular. It made me slightly dizzy, although I had consumed two beers at lunch, and this might have had something to do with it.

In the car, Maria asked to see the photographs of Larry and the Lincoln Navigator. I fished them out of the briefcase and handed them to her. Then she said "Where's the money?"

"Money?"

199

"You said you had a lot, plenty of cash, didn't you say that?"

The money was in a manila envelope in the tote I had purchased in Manhattan Beach a hundred years ago. Wrinkled hundred-dollar bills in stacks; ransom money. I handed the envelope to her. She counted out a big chunk of it.

I said "How much is that?"

"Five grand."

"For what?"

"Just sit tight. This is what you wanted."

She got out of the car and walked back toward Miramon's office, money in one hand, photographs in the other. But she didn't walk up the stairs; she went into the cleaners. Two minutes later she emerged, walked back to the car and got in. She handed me a slip of paper.

"What's this?"

"Your claim check."

"What?"

"From the cleaners."

"For what?"

"I don't know. He handed it to me. The guy behind the counter."

"You gave him that money?" I thought of Alex Miramon's Cheshire grin and felt my dizziness return.

"Yes."

"Five grand?" I made a motion to get out of the car. She grabbed my wrist.

"You can't go back now," she said. "He told me it won't be ready till Friday."

37

Now Murray wanted his car back. I would have expected that the money I gave him would be good for more than a couple of day's worth of his Mercury Marquis. Murray did not dispute this; he would return the car, but he needed it to drive to the ball game. There was no way, he claimed, to get from Marina del Rey to Chavez Ravine, where the stadium was located, except by car. I could have it back after that.

The Dodgers were so far out of play you'd need the Hubble space telescope to find them. Scalpers couldn't give the tickets away, but Murray had a seat that night right over the home team dugout, on the third base line, and he couldn't let it go to waste.

I said "You want to see them lose another game? It's like watching paint dry."

"I like to go to the ballpark, Tom. Since I was a kid. I eat a hot dog. I sing the National Anthem. We used to go to all the Dodgers' home games. Baseball was like a religion to us."

"You still eat those Dodger Dogs?" This particular sacrament was indigestible, but Murray was not so easily discouraged.

"You're not gonna give me back my car?"

I told Murray to take a cab and meet me at Frankenstein's Quality Cars, and asked him to stop off at my boat first, to pick up a few things I needed.

I said "Drive around a little before you go to Al's. If somebody follows you, go home and come back later. I'll wait for you."

The camper was still there. Al Frankenstein was busy in his little office, filling out some papers with a customer. He tossed me the keys and told me to try and get it back to him in one piece. Murray was waiting across the street, where I had parked the Marquis. He claimed that nobody had followed his cab. We agreed that I had overpaid him for the use of his car, but I thought it would be best if I left a little credit at the store. It was hard to anticipate, just then, what I might need. He handed me what I had asked him to bring, and left.

I drove the camper up Pacific Coast Highway to a supermarket in Trancas, where I took on supplies. I called Larry's office on one of my new cell phones and spent some time in idle conversation with somebody who obviously had been left with instructions to keep me on the line as long as possible. I made it easy for him, talking about that night's ball game.

Then Santa Barbara, where it is not legal to sleep in your camper if it is parked on a public street, but it can be done if you're tricky about it.

I spent the next morning reading back issues of the *Santa Barbara News-Press* on microfiche. For the last year or so the city had experienced a surge in drug-related crimes and accidental drug overdoses. High-quality heroin and cocaine were cheap and plentiful. The University of California at Santa Barbara was right outside of town, and regret was expressed that college students might have access to these potent drugs. As if they needed any help. I stood on the sidewalk outside the newspaper offices and called the reporter who had written most of the stories. We made a date to meet for a sandwich on State Street later that morning. Then I heard the toreador theme from *Carmen* again. This time the call was from Lou Gizzi.

I said "How'd you get this number?"

"Your friend's phone. When we called you from the taxi?"

"Oh. You're at the store?"

"Yeah."

"OK, go find a phone boot and call me back."

I terminated the call. It's hard to stop saying 'phone boot' once you get in the habit. I found a stone bench on the sidewalk, and settled in.

"OK, I hadda close the store. You satisfied?"

"You called me, Lou."

"I wanna ask you something. It's kinda sensitive." I said nothing. "We did you a favor, right?"

I said "I don't remember. It's been hectic."

"You don't remember me telling you how the SUV scam went down? How your buddy hung you out to dry?"

"I remember."

Lou said "Alright. Now, you go to the classes and they've got FBI guys right outside. They come inside, we throw them out. They think somebody's gonna tell secrets in a cooking class cause the name of the place is Cosa Nostra. It's a joke. Meanwhile it keeps them busy."

"So?"

"So they gotta ask you what do we do at the classes. What do you tell them?"

"I tell them they're cooking classes."

"They ever ask you to wear a wire?"

"Yeah. Once."

"You wore it?"

204

"No."

"Where are you now?"

"Ask me a different question."

"Alright, but I think maybe I know, and some friends of mine are asking me how are things there?"

"Look, I've got a lunch meeting."

"Fine. Enjoy your lunch. But your friend wants you off the streets for a reason. You know something, and we're wondering what it is."

"Yeah. Me too."

So that was the payback, the reason Lou Gizzi had called me on the sand at Manhattan Beach to tell me Larry Hayden had betrayed me. Now I was to betray Larry. Lou had 'friends' who wanted to know what Larry was up to, and I could tell them plenty. I could tell them Wheelchair Jack and Homeland Security were working undercover for the Government, that Larry's people had been supplying them with cut-rate drugs to sell, first to Cossi and, after Los Angeles had him killed for refusing to share the wealth, to whoever took Cossi's place.

I also knew Larry's style, which was completely standard. First you get the connection going, then increase the size of the payloads until you plan one that's large enough to attract the big fish. That one's the sting and everybody gets arrested. You don't get the people at the very top. There's not enough dope in the world to get the biggest guys to do naughty things on a beach in Santa Barbara County at night, but you had a reasonable chance of attracting middle management. Federal sentencing standards were severe enough to encourage these mokes to testify against their bosses.

So. But there was no way I was going to sing in Lou Gizzi's ear. The idea nauseated me. So far I had been feckless, foolish, trusting and a general dim-bulb ever since the MasterCard lady down South had called to tell me I had bought the Lincoln. But I didn't see myself as anybody's stooge. Larry needed payback, no question about it. But I thought I could accomplish this without becoming an accomplice to somebody

205

else's crime. With a little imagination I could commit crimes of my own.

*　　*　　*

If State Street were any prettier it would be a set for a Twilight Zone episode. Rod Serling would slide out from behind a potted *ficus benjamini* and say 'Strange as it seems, these ordinary Americans have no idea they are living in the most beautiful place in the known universe.'

The last time I was on State Street, Maria had been with me, and I missed her this time. But I wanted to be free to do any stupid or reckless thing I felt like doing. It was clear that I had nothing left to lose. I was still angry enough, and I wanted to be able to express this rare bloody-mindedness freely, without thought that I might endanger Maria.

Newspaper reporters don't drink anymore. It's disappointing. No more belts of rye in Dixie cups to help harried reporters meet deadlines. We sat at an outside table. Herb Wander had an iced tea with his little salad. He and Lee Brown would have made perfect lunch companions. He was young, had a sparse beard, and wore rimless John Lennon glasses behind which he blinked a lot. He wore a crystal on a silver chain around his neck. He wanted proof I wasn't making stuff up. Apparently people do that a lot with reporters. I told him Santa Barbara was up to its gills in high-quality heroin and cocaine, and that people were dying from it. He knew that. I told him the traffic was being managed by a guy called Wheelchair Jack and his friend, a black bodybuilder. He wrote this down but did not look impressed. I told him these men worked for the US Government. That got his attention.

He said "You can prove that?"

I told him I was a fugitive, that I had assaulted Homey and was liable to be arrested for it. This information caused Herb Wander to wilt. He nibbled on some lettuce then took off his glasses and started polishing them on the tablecloth. He had decided I was crazy.

I told him that tomorrow night a big drug delivery would go down at Point Sal, that it would be the Government delivering the drugs, and that the purpose was to take down the Mafia leadership in Southern California. I hoped I was right.

Herb Wander did not seem to react to the idea that the Government might be supplying Santa Barbara's drug users. He took a few more notes, but was more interested in UC Santa Barbara coeds, who kept walking by our table in surprisingly revealing clothing. Girls keep getting nakeder as I get older.

I told Herb Wander that if any of what I had told him was communicated to any agent of the US Government, the deal would likely be called off, and that he should tell someone at the Santa Barbara County Sheriff's Department to set up some surveillance and some firepower at Point Sal Beach Friday night. I told him that some of the people they might arrest would cop to being Federal agents and the whole thing would be over, including the worst part of Santa Barbara's drug problem. I wondered if he believed any of it. It even sounded nuts to me.

What did I have to lose? I figured if Larry's careful plans went up the pipe his drug-dealing days would be over; maybe his career, too, and he'd probably have to leave me alone. And anyway, heroin and cocaine are bad for people. I was on the right side of the issues.

I spent an hour in a cell phone store a block from where I had eaten lunch with Herb Wander. Yes, the very newest ones had a GPS chip that worked like the emergency locator in an EPIRB, the gadget you toss in the water when your ship is sinking, which broadcasts your exact location using the Global Positioning Satellite. You see, what if you had an emergency and called 911 and they couldn't locate you in a hurry? With the newest cell phone it was no problem; the GPS chip tells the people at 911 exactly where you are. As Alex Miramon had warned me, persons who do not want to be found should not buy such a phone. It was a beautiful phone, a futuristic handful of chrome all folded up like a Pismo clam.

*   *   *

The next morning I drove up to Lompoc and got the Lincoln Navigator out of impound; a sweaty few minutes for me, but the cop in the kiosk barely looked at the papers I showed him. The bullet holes were there, three I could count, but evidently no vital parts had been damaged. The beast started up and ran just fine, I turned on the radio and learned that the missile launch scheduled for that night had been cancelled.

I was driving the Lincoln! It had driven me crazy and I was going to get even; with the car, with Larry Hayden, with anyone else who happened to be nearby. Maria had said flame throwers were not my style, but I'd learned a lot since then. Not that I thought I could actually get my hands on one. A flame thrower, that is. Right then I was confident I could figure something out that would be at least as destructive. And it was Friday. If I believed what the man in the drycleaners had told Maria, the Lincoln was now *embrujado*, cursed, under a spell. Good. It just went in the mix with everything else. I stepped down hard on the gas. The Lincoln roared. It felt like a dream. There was only one place to go.

I parked at a scenic spot overlooking the ocean, and called Larry. As I waited for him to come to the phone I took a couple of deep breaths. It would be important to get exactly the right blend of hurt feelings and hysteria.

Larry said "Change your mind about coming in?"

"You prick."

'What?"

"You're a prick. You got Cossi's people at the dealership to sell the Lincoln Navigator to me, on a fake credit card you helped them set up."

"Tom, I-"

"-You ruined my life."

"Where are you getting this crap?"

"Cooking class."

"What?"

"Cooking class. The guys told me. Gizzi and Cannizzarro."

Silence. Then he said "Where are you?"

"Lompoc. And if you've been wondering about the tape I made in the restaurant, forget it. It's right here in my pocket." I patted my pocket for emphasis.

Silence.

"And I've got the car."

"You've got-"

"-The Lincoln Navigator. Maria's lawyer got a Court Order releasing it, so I went and got it. I'm driving it. Now."

Silence.

"Larry, you are thoroughly screwed." I considered telling him he was *embrujado* as well as screwed but I thought it would take too long to explain, and who would believe such a thing, anyway?

38

I bought a pair of hiking boots. I bought a sleeping bag in a camouflage design, a canteen and a light backpack; the kind that day hikers use. I found a pair of 7X50 binoculars in a pawnshop. I put my newly-purchased gear in the back of the Lincoln. I left the camper in a public parking lot, taking from it only my newest cell phone and the little stainless steel 20-gauge shotgun Murray had brought from my boat. I had bought the shotgun a few years ago. The guy who sold it to me had said it was the ideal weapon to ward off pirates at sea. The pirates never appeared. The weapon had been sleeping peacefully in the forepeak for many years.

I bought a box of rounds for the shotgun; slugs, not shotshells. I gassed up the Lincoln and bought five more gallons of gas in a red plastic can. Then I drove down to Point

Sal Beach State Park.

I let some air out of the tires, then drove past the parking area and down onto the sand. The surf was up. I could see no one. I parked the Lincoln just below the high water mark, assembled my gear, and abandoned ship; doors unlocked. I left the gas can on the front seat. I kept the keys.

I hiked back up the road a mile or two. New boots a little stiff. It was a nice morning for it; cool and hazy. When I thought I had gained enough altitude I left the road and walked back through the brush in a more or less westerly direction. After another mile or so I found myself looking down on Point Sal Beach. I was on a ridge about a hundred feet above the beach. It was steep and brushy all the way down. I was in that vacant state of mind you can get into outdoors, if the place is wild enough and you are alone. Out in front of me was the Pacific Ocean.

There was still nobody on the beach. No vessels in the anchorage. The Lincoln looked lonely; maybe it sensed its fate. This was the end of the road.

I had rediscovered my bottle of Xanax in the camper, and I took two with a swig of water from my canteen. The life of an outdoorsman. My only problem was finding a level spot to set up the sleeping bag so that I wouldn't roll down the bluff while trying to use it. I listened to the sea birds and dozed.

When I awoke there was a trawler in the anchorage and several cars in the parking lot. It was just beginning to get dark. A bank of fog was approaching from seaward. Binoculars revealed nobody on deck on the trawler, three or four people standing on the beach.

Much discussion and pointing at the Lincoln. Nobody seemed willing to go near it, and I had the feeling it worried them. Join the club.

There were some lights on the water, but whatever vessels they were on were invisible in the mist. The tide had come up and the surf was now only a few feet from the Lincoln. Big breakers hit the sand one after another, making a lot of noise. Another car arrived and parked, disgorging two more people who joined the group already on the beach. I was reminded of the crowd of spectators on the same beach the morning Maria and I were arrested. They seemed to project the same sense of anticipation. What's going to happen now? Anyway, that's what I was feeling.

Now there was activity on the trawler. Crew members had picked up a bright yellow inflatable raft with a block and tackle, and were lowering it into the water.

My new cell phone rang, scaring me badly. I had forgotten it was there. I let it ring a few times until I felt composed enough to answer.

"Hi Larry. Nice of you to call." I had stopped asking where people were getting my number.

"Tom," he said, "you've got to come in. You have no idea how much trouble you're in."

"I'm not the only one."

"Huh?"

"Right now, the Point Sal deal is blown."

"What deal?"

"Save your breath. I'm right here on the beach watching. Santa Barbara heat are on the job."

"Look, I-"

"-Gotta go."

I left the connection open and threw the phone down to the beach. I tried to get it close to the Lincoln but it was too dark to see where it landed. I figured Larry's next call would be to the trawler, to tout them off the delivery. I may have been right. In about ten minutes the aft deck of the trawler was brightly illuminated. Someone was on the control bridge and I could hear the engines start. The yellow raft that had just been launched was now being picked up again. I held up the key gadget for the Lincoln, remembering how the salesman had called it a 'keyless remote entry system and panic button,' and pressed the panic button. The Lincoln's headlights started to flash on and off and the car alarm started to wail. We've all

212

heard these alarms on the street, but at Point Sal, in the gathering dark, the effect was almost Biblical.

Shots were fired from the trawler. Then shooting that seemed to be coming from the beach. I thought, who do you shoot at in the dark? then remembered that it hadn't stopped Maria. I had the impression people were shooting at the Lincoln. Then I realized that I had told Larry I was driving the Lincoln, so that was where he would have figured me to be; in the car. That's where literal-minded thinking will get you. Then the Lincoln started to burn. Burning and flashing and wailing; you really had to be there.

Then two helicopters appeared over the ridge from the southeast and hovered over the beach. Onboard loudspeakers announced the presence of the police; throw down your weapons, lie flat on the ground. Point Sal Beach State Park had been busted. The Lincoln was now fully engaged in flames. The headlights had gone out, or maybe had been shot out, but it still wailed. The effect was downright spooky, a sort of automotive Guernica. Far, far better than I had imagined it would be.

Through the binoculars, I thought I could see Larry Hayden at the control bridge on the trawler, just like in my dream. He had some kind of firearm in his hand and he seemed to be pointing it at me. Reflexively, I picked up the 20-gauge and tried to line him up in the gunsight. It would have been an impossible shot. But, just as I had dreamed it, I saw Larry take two rounds in the chest and fall out of the control bridge into the water. Again.

39

"I didn't shoot him."

Maria said "Are you sure?"

"I told you. I never even loaded the shotgun."

"How do you know it wasn't loaded when Murray brought it to you?"

I rolled over in bed to look at her. "Nobody keeps a loaded shotgun around. It's not safe."

There were storm winds blowing, making *Den Mother's* docklines groan. Occasionally she would heel over a little, responding to a strong gust. Loose rigging snapped and crackled on sailboats all around us.

Maria said "Did you ever look and see?"

"See what?"

"If it was loaded."

I didn't remember if I had ever done that.

I said "It doesn't matter. I sniffed the barrel. It hadn't been fired."

She said "You sniffed it?"

"Isn't that how to tell if it's been fired?"

She giggled. "You'll shoot your nose off."

The wind increased. Den Mother rolled. Forward, in the galley, something clanked in the dark.

I said "I'm not even sure he was there."

"Larry?"

"A couple days after I got back I called his office and they said he was out sick. Lee Brown says he heard he had fallen down a flight of stairs in the Federal Building and broken his collarbone."

Maria said "They're not trying to arrest you anymore?"

"Lee called. Nobody in the US Attorney's Office ever heard of me, and the Department of Homeland Security refused to give him any information. Lee told them if they wanted me, to call him and he'd bring me in."

"Do you think they will?"

"Not unless everyone wants to hear what really happened at Point Sal that night. By the time it got into the papers it was a story about a bunch of people arrested for discharging firearms in a State park."

"You're kidding."

"Well, somebody is. Larry's people scooped the whole thing up and buried it in the backyard somewhere."

"The Lincoln, too?"

"Physically, I don't know. Want to take a ride up there with me and find out?"

She gave me a stony look.

I said "It could be up there on the beach, a burned-out wreck with the surf washing over it, but in a larger sense, it disappeared."

Suddenly we heard it start to rain, a short, furious burst like ball bearings hitting the salon hardtop. Somewhere out in the Pacific there was serious weather working down on us. Maria turned and pressed herself tightly against my back, tucking the covers in around us. This sort of thing is fun anywhere, but on a boat, in bad weather, it's like a dream.

"I thought it would be a good idea to make a police report. You know, I'm the guy that drove the sucker out of impound, and then later it gets shot full of holes and burned. I thought it would be best to report it vandalized and torched before somebody decided I had something to do with it."

She said "Yes. Good thinking. So did you report it?"

"I tried. I called the Highway Patrol, but as soon as I told them when and where it happened, they said it was out of their hands and I should call the Department of Homeland Security."

"Did you call them?"

"You must be joking. I called MasterCard. According to the computer, the account is closed. The balance due is zero."

Maria said "Does anybody know what really happened?"

I recalled the image of Larry Hayden, shot in the chest, falling off the trawler into the water. Twice. If he broke his collarbone I'd settle for it.

"Well," I said, "there are several versions. I think it depends on who you ask."

"Are you going to go up there and get my Magnum back?"

"No."

Maria sniffed, turned so she was facing away from me, and very ostentatiously went to sleep. I lay in bed and listened to the wind blow.

-    -   -

RECIPES DEMONSTRATED BY CHEF VICTOR CANNIZZARRO AT LA COSA NOSTRA COOKING SCHOOL - BRENTWOOD, CALIFORNIA

(In the order in which they appear in the book)

Spigola Alla Procidana

(Striped Bass with Red Wine Vinegar and Mint)

Serves 4

8 tablespoons olive oil
2 cups red wine vinegar
2 cups dry white wine
3 teaspoons dried basil
1 teaspoon dried oregano
Salt and pepper
4 10-ounce striped bass filets
8 or more whole fresh mint leaves

The way to buy the striped bass filets is to buy whole fish and have the counter man filet them on the spot, leaving the skin on. Avoid buying filets that were cut at some time in the past. They get unhappy sitting around the fish store. Before you cook them, run your finger around the edges of the filets. Often, a few scales will remain. Striped bass scales are very large and hard and you do not want to eat them.

In a shallow baking dish combine the olive oil, vinegar, wine and spices. Place the bass filets in the pan and place two or three mint leaves on each. Broil in a preheated oven. If you know what you're doing and want to get tricky you can try cooking the filets skin side down and not turning them over. If this scares you, at least do most of your broiling on the skin side, and turn them over very briefly, to get a finish on the tops. When the filets are done, place them on a serving platter and pour on the sauce. Decorate with additional mint leaves.

Giardiniera

(Marinated vegetables)

You can use any kind of vegetables you want, except maybe lettuce. I never tried lettuce. It seems like it would get too floppy.

Cut the vegetables into bite-sized pieces. You want to get artistic, go ahead. You can use a *mandoline* to do crinkle-cuts on cucumber, carrots and so on. Blanche and shock the pieces in separate batches, then dry them and place them in a glass jar and cover with white wine vinegar. Marinate overnight. These are perfect for antipasto

Frittata Fredda alla Rustica

(Spinach - Parmesan Frittata)

Serves 4 to 6

This is kind of like a small omelet, highly seasoned. Italians eat them for breakfast in little sandwiches called panini. You can also slice them into wedges for antipasto. I'd like to tell you that my mother made these, but she worked full time cutting patterns in a dress factory and didn't have time to cook much.

6 large eggs
Salt and Pepper
Grated nutmeg
4 cups loosely packed spinach leaves, rinsed, dried
  and finely chopped.
1 cup grated Parmigiano-Reggiano cheese
1 tablespoon olive oil

In a bowl combine the eggs, salt, pepper, nutmeg, spinach leaves and half the grated cheese. Beat lightly.

Heat the oil in an omelet pan. Make sure the entire inside of the pan is coated with oil. When hot, add the egg mixture. Cook at a low heat, stirring the upper portion of the frittata, but leaving the bottom to set. After about four minutes the mixture should be brown at the bottom and not quite firm in the center. The top should remain semi-liquid. Loosen the frittata at the edges with a spatula. Distribute the remaining cheese over the top. Place the omelet pan in a fast broiler until the frittata is lightly browned on top. This should take about two minutes. Then remove it from the broiler and let it cool for a few minutes. Cover the pan with a plate and invert the frittata onto the plate. Serve at room temperature.

To be honest with you, this is a difficult dish to do right. Don't be discouraged if you mess up the first few times.

Suppli

(Filled rice balls)

Serves 6

2 cups arborio rice
1 cup tomato sauce
1½ cups water
2 tablespoons butter
2 ounces grated Parmigiano-Reggiano cheese
2 large eggs, beaten
1 cup breadcrumbs
2 cups olive oil (used to be lard, but these days people shriek when they hear the word)

Fillings:
Any combination of the following, chopped fine.
Mushrooms
Onions
prosciutto
fresh herbs
cooked chicken livers/giblets
lean veal
mozzarella

Prepare risotto in the traditional way, adding the tomato sauce at the end. Remove from heat and add the butter

221

and grated cheese. Stir. Turn the risotto out onto a plate and put in refrigerator for at least two hours. At this time it will be very thick.

Prepare the filling of your choice. Prepare a bowl with the two beaten eggs, and a tray of breadcrumbs. Take a small amount of rice in the palm of your wet hand, flatten the rice and place in the center a teaspoonful of the filling. Close your hand and form the rice into a ball, making sure the filling is securely closed inside. The resulting ball should be about twice the size of a walnut. Roll it in the beaten eggs, then the breadcrumbs. Deep fry in olive oil until they are golden brown and crunchy. Serve immediately.

Aringa Marinata

(Marinated herring)

Pommery mustard
Mayonnaise
Lemon juice
Cayenne pepper
Pickled herring, sliced thin (1/4 inch)
Romaine lettuce
Lemon slices

Mix one part mayonnaise to two parts mustard. Add a small amount of lemon juice and cayenne pepper to taste. Add the herring and toss well.

Serve on a bed of lettuce, garnished with the lemon slices.

Spaghetti con Fegatini di Pollo

(Spaghetti and chicken livers)

Serves 4 to 6

2 cups butter or olive oil
2 pounds chicken livers, cut in half
1 pound spaghetti
juice of 2 lemon
6 tablespoons dry white wine
1 teaspoon chopped fresh basil

Saute the chicken livers in the butter or oil at a high heat until browned. Add the wine, lemon juice and basil and cook another 2 or 3 minutes. Cook the spaghetti in salted boiling water until it is *al dente*. Drain the spaghetti and place in a serving bowl. Pour the chicken livers and sauce over the spaghetti and toss lightly.

Aragosta Piccante

(Spicy lobster)

Serves 4

2 2-pound lobsters
¼ cup olive oil
¾ cup chopped shallots
4 garlic cloves, chopped
2 cup dry red wine
1 cup chicken broth
4 tablespoons tomato paste
1 tablespoon chopped fresh rosemary
1 tablespoon crushed red pepper flakes
1 tablespoon chopped fresh sage
¼ cup chopped fresh parsley
Ground black pepper
2 tablespoons vinegar

First you have to kill the lobsters. I'm sorry, but there's no way around this. They have to be alive when you buy them. Nobody would buy a dead lobster, and there's a very good reason for this. Have the counter man take the lobsters out of the tank and put them on a flat surface. They should raise up their claws like little prizefighters ready to go in the ring.

We are not boiling these lobsters, so you can't just look the other way and heave them into a pot of boiling water. No, you have to kill them. If it bothers you, forget lobsters and open a can of pork and beans. I use a cleaver, and give them a good whack to the head. Takes a minute. You get used to it. But it's not for everybody, and sometimes people will walk out of my classes when they see me do it. Classes they've paid for, but never mind.

Crack open the shells at the claws, the legs and tails.

Heat the oil in a large skillet and cook the lobster pieces for 10 to 12 minutes. Add the stock, the wine, the vinegar the shallots and garlic, reduce heat and continue to cook for an additional 10 minutes. Add the tomato paste, rosemary, sage, black pepper, and crushed red pepper flakes, cover and cook for an additional five minutes, then remove the lobster pieces and reduce the sauce at a low heat for 20 minutes or so, until it thickens.

Use shears to open the claws, legs and tails, but leave the meat in place. On a platter, arrange the lobster pieces in the form of a lobster, cover with sauce and sprinkle with the chopped parsley.

Crostata alla Marmellata

(Marmalade tart)
Serves 8

1 ¾ cups white flour
2 cups sugar
8 tablespoons butter, at room temperature
2 teaspoons grated lemon rind
1 egg
2 to 3 tablespoons heavy cream
1 cup marmalade
1 teaspoon Grand Marnier

Mix together the flour, sugar and lemon rind. Cut the butter into small pieces and mix it with the flour with a pastry blender, two forks, your fingers or the paddle attachment of a mixer, until the mixture resembles coarse meal or sand. Make a hollow, or well, in the mixture and add the egg yolk, then the cream, slowly working them into the flour mixture. Gather the dough into a ball, and place on a lightly floured cool work surface. Roll it out into a nine-inch circle. The dough should be approximately ¼ inch thick. Fit the dough into a lightly buttered nine-inch tart pan with a removable bottom. Refrigerate for at least one hour.

Heat the marmalade and Grand Marnier slowly until it is smooth, then remove from heat.

Place a circle of aluminum foil in the bottom of the tart pan, and weigh down with pie weights or dry beans. Place the pan in a preheated 400 degree oven and bake for 20 minutes, then remove the foil and weights and bake for another 20 minutes. Remove from oven and add the marmalade filling. Bake an additional 10 minutes. Allow time for the tart to cool before attempting to remove it from the pan.

Cassata Alla Siciliana
(Pound cake with ricotta and chocolate)

Serves 8

3 tablespoons Marsala wine
1 can pitted dark sweet cherries
1 pint ricotta cheese
¼ cup white sugar
2 tablespoons heavy cream
1 pound cake (approx. 12 oz.)
12 oz. semisweet chocolate
¼ cup mixed candied citrus peel, chopped
¼ cup Marsala wine
1 cup sweet butter

This is a traditional Italian recipe from a time when fat was good and nobody went on a diet unless maybe they were sick or too poor to buy food. Probably, this cake should have a warning label.

Drain cherries and cut into small pieces. Reserve the syrup.

Mix together the ricotta, sugar, 3 tablespoons Marsala wine, and whipping cream. Beat until smooth, then add cherries and candied citrus peel.

Cut the pound cake lengthwise twice, creating three layers. Spread half the filling on the bottom layer. Cover with second layer and spread remaining filling, then top with the third and final layer.

To make the frosting, melt the chocolate, cherry syrup,

227

butter and ¼ cup Marsala in the top of a double boiler over simmering water. Stir. Remove from heat and place in refrigerator. Stir every 15 minutes until it is smooth and firm.

Cover the entire cake with ¼ inch of frosting. Use a narrow cake spatula, dipping occasionally in hot water.

Serve at room temperature. Keeps well in the refrigerator.

Arrosto di Vitello

(Roast stuffed loin of veal)

Serves 10 to 12

2 cups bread crumbs
3 pounds Italian sweet sausage, pureed
3 eggs, beaten
12 sage leaves, chopped
Salt and pepper
1 8-to-9 pound veal loin,
    butterflied and pounded thin with a mallet
12 slices prosciutto
1 cup olive oil
2 onions chopped
2 celery stalks chopped
1 bunch carrots chopped
8 cups dry white wine
8 cups veal stock
8 sage leaves

In a large bowl combine the milk, breadcrumbs, sausage, eggs, sage and parsley. Add salt and pepper to taste.

Lay out the veal loin flat, and season the entire inside with salt and pepper. Cover half the inside of the loin with half the prosciutto. Place the stuffing over the prosciutto and cover it with the remaining prosciutto. Roll the loin lengthwise into a bundle and tie with string.

Preheat oven to 350 f. Heat the oil in a large heavy shallow roasting pan. Place the celery, onions and carrots over the bottom of the pan and place the loin on top. Roast for approx. 45 minutes, basting with the wine and stock until it is used up.

Remove the loin from the pan, strain out the vegetables, puree them, and add them back to the pan juices. Heat. Add remaining sage leaves and salt and pepper to taste.

Slice the loin thinly and serve with the sauce.

Cacciucco alla Livornese

(Fish stew with capers)

Serves 4

2 cups olive oil
3 garlic cloves, peeled
¼ cup red wine vinegar
¼ cup dry white wine
Salt and pepper
3 cups marinara sauce
1 tablespoon capers, drained
1 tablespoon fresh basil leaves, chopped
1 teaspoon fresh rosemary leaves. Chopped

2 tablespoons fresh parsley leaves, chopped
1 Two pound lobster
10 littleneck clams
14 mussels, washed and debearded
1 pound fish (can be any mild white fish) cut in bite-
   sized pieces
10 medium shrimp, shelled and deveined
2 medium squid, cleaned and sliced into thin rings

In a skillet combine the marinara sauce, rosemary, capers, basil and half the parsley. Cook five minutes at low heat.

Place the lobster, mussels and clams in a roasting pan and pour the sauce over them. Cover and cook at medium heat for 15 minutes on stove top.

Transfer a cup of the sauce from the roasting pan to a skillet and add the fish, shrimp and squid. Cover and cook briefly at low heat.

Add the contents of the skillet to the roasting pan and bake the combined contents for 10 minutes at 425 degrees.

Remove from oven. Crack the lobster claws, legs and tail. Place the seafood on a platter and garnish with the sauce and the remaining parsley.

- - - - - - - - - -

About the Author

Jonathan Schwartz was born in Washington DC. After graduating from Bard College and the University of Pennsylvania Law School he went on to work in Washington, DC for the Federal Trade Commission and, later, the Department of Commerce.

He ultimately made the decision to accept an SEC position in Los Angeles, and decided to make Southern California his home.

He now lives and practices law in Marina del Rey, California, where his private law practice is limited exclusively to securities regulation, disputes between broker-dealers and customers, securities fraud, and enforcement.

He worked his way through college as a professional musician and has performed stand-up comedy at numerous venues in the Los Angeles area.

All three novels featuring Attorney Tom McGuire are now available through Amazon.com at **www.legalmystery.com**

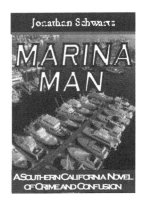  

Made in the USA
Lexington, KY
06 December 2016